Fighting My Fate

Copyright

First Edition, February 2023
Copyright © 2023 by Melony Ann

Paperback ISBN: 978-1-961966-60-4

Published by: Carxander Publishing
Minnesota

Opening Quote

He's a phone call to his parents. He's a Bible by the bed. He's the t-shirt that I'm wearin'. He's the song stuck in my head. He's solid, and he's steady. Like the Allegheny runs. He knows just where he's goin'. And he's proud of where he's from. One of the good ones. He's one of the good ones. A love me like he should one. Like he wrote the book one. The kind you find when you don't even look one. Anybody can be good once. But he's good all the time. He's one of the good ones. And he's all mine.

The Good Ones by Gabby Barrett

Chapter One

☙ Dane ☙

"You may kiss your bride!" the officiant says.

Everyone in the room stands. We all clap and hoot and holler. Alex Lucinio wastes no time sweeping his new wife, Raleigh, into his arms. He lifts her and kisses her as he runs with her up the aisle. A chorus of cheers and laughter echoes through the room. It's been three years since the two of them met. Their happily ever after was hard earned, but fuck do they deserve it.

"It's so weird seeing a billionaire not put on something lavish," Skyla Winters, the beautiful blond standing in front of me, says.

I smile and fight to kiss her plump red lips. "Alex has never been into doing it bigger and better. And Raleigh hates attention."

I look around the event room at the Chicago Winery. It's the perfect place for them to hold their wedding. The floors are hardwood. The chairs match. It looks a little bit like a modernized version of the ballroom of an ancient castle. Bricks along the wall. Wood to accent. It's beautiful. I can see exactly why Alex and Raleigh chose it. It matches their personalities to a tee. Modern, yet classic and old fashioned. Billionaires, but not the kind that flaunt it.

The wedding party follows behind the newly married couple. They're going to get pictures taken. The rest of us are to head out to the terrace to drink and be merry.

Skyla takes my hand and tugs me with her towards the outdoor terrace. She was promised some kind of delectable appetizers. I've learned not to get in the way of this woman and her food. Where she puts it is a whole other thing I haven't unraveled the mystery of. She can eat, but she's skinny, almost too skinny. She's somewhere around five-feet-one, though, so many would think it all goes hand in hand. She's short so she should be small. I disagree. I've always wondered if there's more to it. Not that I think she has an eating disorder. I just don't know what it could be.

Not like she doesn't have enough stress to deal with. She's the Chief Financial Officer of Lucinio Tech, Alex's multi-billion dollar security technology company. That's not all, though. She came from a pretty fucked up situation. We looked into her background enough to find out she was pushed out of her last job because the CEO didn't like that she wouldn't lay down for him and take him beating the shit out of her daily.

She still fears he's coming for her. Even though she knows the level of power this family wields. Josh Lucinio, Alex's twin brother, is the leader of Lucinio Mafia. We're legit. Legal. But we cross lines and spend a lot of time in the darkness so the innocent people of this world don't have to. Vigilante justice.

I say we because I'm just as much a part of it as they are. Josh and Alex are my half brothers. We share a mother. I'm a Lieutenant with the Chicago Police Department. I run my own taskforce dealing with major crimes. But I also run missions right alongside my brothers. It's an outlet I didn't know I needed, and one Josh never believed he'd allow.

I'm definitely not a model cop. Not that I'd ever treat anyone poorly. I don't have a single strike against me for being a dick to anyone I've dealt with on the streets. All of my strikes come from the fact that I have a real problem with authority. It's probably the biggest reason I was pulled onto Taylor Reddick's taskforce in the first place.

Taylor is another Lieutenant with Chicago PD. He got his own taskforce a while ago and handpicked me to help him run it. When he pulled me in, we barely knew each other, but we'd hit it off immediately because of how alike we were. He had just as big of an issue with authority. Especially when he saw them fucking up. They don't like being called out on shit. It's a wonder Taylor and I haven't been fired. Not that I don't know the reason for that. It's fully because of our connections.

Despite running different taskforces now, Taylor and I are still as close as ever. He works closer with Ryan Crane, the leader of the Crane Mafia, than he does with Josh, but over the past few years, the two mafia families have not only aligned, but also joined resources. Between the two families, we could dominate the entire world.

And we do. Josh and Ryan are the reason Taylor and I are where we are. We know it as well as all of the Administration assholes we deal with at the department.

"Oh my God, Dane." Skyla looks up at me, her big blue eyes shining like diamonds. She holds up something with a toothpick sticking out of it. "You have to try it."

I raise an eyebrow and move my head back. "What is it? It smells like something waiting to kill me."

She giggles, and fuck if my dick doesn't get hard at the sound. "I thought so, too, but you have to taste it. I don't know what it is."

I groan but take the toothpick. I give it a sniff and then shove it in my mouth without a second thought as Skyla watches me with a giant smile that lights up her whole face. I chew quickly before slowing down when the flavors hit my tongue.

"Huh," I say thoughtfully, "Well, it's definitely tuna with a pickle chip and black olive, but what the hell is it seasoned with?" I grab another one and pop it into my mouth.

"Honey barbecue sauce for sure." Skyla follows my lead and eats another one.

"Got that, but there's some kind of a rub on it."

"Oh my God, it's so good." She takes my hand again and drags me down the line of hors d'oeuvres. I chuckle as she grabs almost everything.

"Not a fan of caviar?" I ask when she avoids it like the plague.

She wrinkles her nose in the most adorable way possible. "No. Eew."

I laugh because I don't blame her. Something about caviar makes me want to chuck it across the room and watch it slide down the wall.

"This wedding is putting ideas in Harleigh's head," Gavin rumbles from behind me.

I smile and look back at him. "Aren't you supposed to be getting fancy pictures taken?"

"Shh… I escaped. I'm fucking starving."

I laugh. "Not gonna lie. I'm glad he just had you and Josh up there with him. I've never been more grateful he's so low-key."

"Asshole." Gavin shoves me playfully with a grin before he catches a glimpse of his own fiancé, Harleigh. "I'm gonna take her some of this. She's starving."

"I heard no one in the wedding party eats anything until dinner."

"I thought that was a myth, but fuck. Mark it as true. No one has had time to eat." Gavin slips away as quickly as he appeared.

He and Harleigh are next in line to get married. In fact, their wedding is right around the corner. I'm a little surprised they haven't already done it, though. It's not like either of them have commitment issues or cold feet. They're very much in love. I think the wait has always been out of respect for Alex and Raleigh. They got engaged first. They should get married first. At least in Gavin's mind. He's always been like that. It's why he makes such a good second in command in the Lucinio Mafia. Despite how ruthless he can be, it's mainly because of his need to make sure everyone around him is taken care of. We'd all take a bullet for each other, but I think he takes it a step beyond that.

"This place is gorgeous," someone with a deep voice and southern accent says from behind me.

"Oh! Lyric is sitting with DJ. I'm going to talk to her." Skyla beelines with her plate towards a table where a gorgeous dark-haired woman is sitting with a tall, dark, and muscular man.

I chuckle as I turn to the man behind me. "Hey, Matt."

He grins. "Hey, Dane. How's it going?"

I shrug as I finish grabbing my own food. "Same old, same old. How about you?"

"Nice to get out of Gainesville once in a while. Needed a damn break."

"Fuck, I know that feeling."

"Besides, it's cooler up North in the Summer months. Nice reprieve."

I wait for him to finish getting his food, then walk with him to his table. "How's the wife and husband?" Matt is married to both DJ and

Lyric. We've all met and become close through Lyric. She's Josh's ex-girlfriend, but they're still as close as family, so it worked out.

"Life is great. No complaints from me. Lyric has been working hard with Raleigh to get everything ready for the big gala this year."

"The one for the kids worked out so well last year. I'm glad we'll get to do the big one for the adults this year, too. Lance wants to make it an annual thing."

"He's got good reason, being through what he went through. I think it's incredible of him to want to do all of this to help kids who are in the position he was when he was a kid. Cancer's fucking scary shit."

"We're all just happy he's okay."

Matt and I both sit down at the table. Matt sits on the other side of Lyric and puts the plate he filled between them to share. The three of them are adorable together. It makes me wish for what they have. The problem is the only person I've ever actually seen myself with friend-zoned me long ago.

Fuck my life.

"Lyric!" a sweet voice squeals. In a flash, Dallas Cassidy, a delightful and very nice seventeen-year-old friend of the family, has Lyric wrapped in a hug as she slides into her lap.

Lyric lets out an adorable squeak as she hugs her back. "Aren't you supposed to be getting pictures taken?"

Dallas giggles as she helps herself to food off the plate Lyric is sharing with her husbands. "I escaped. I'm starving. Oh my God."

DJ laughs. "If you are, I can't imagine what Josh is feeling."

Dallas blushes a deep shade of red. "He said his stomach is eating itself." She clears her throat. "He's covering for me while I steal something to tide us over." She kisses Lyric's cheek and bounces back up. She uses a napkin as a holder and takes something from each of our plates. She kisses us all on the cheek before she scampers off.

We all can't help but laugh. No one really knows what's going on between her and Josh, but we all know it's something. Josh is thirty-seven, and while we all know he'd never cross lines, we know there's something happening.

Dallas is Josh's best friend's little sister. Alec Cassidy, or Ace, as his crew knows him, is the President of the Viper's Venom, a very ruthless motorcycle crew based here in Chicago but known across the nation.

They're feared even more than the Hells Angels, and they like it that way. No one knows they're just as legal as we are, or that they're as much of vigilantes as us.

As the night drags on, I find myself getting more and more drunk. I love Alex and Raleigh dearly, but shit like this has never been my thing. I'm much more of a go to work, come home, spend time on my own type of man. I like my quiet. I like my solitude. I like the occasional release I get when Josh needs me on a mission.

Mostly though, I like spending time with the woman whose hand has been on my knee for most of the night. Skyla might have classified me as a friend, but it hasn't stopped her pretty face from popping into my head when I'm jerking myself.

Never thought I'd ever be the guy with one-sided feelings. I've always been the one on the opposite side of the spectrum. I don't have a problem getting a woman to make the nights less lonely, but I'm also not one to settle. If it's not working, I don't waste time on it. I'm forty-five. Wasting time isn't an option, and I'm old enough to know better.

The problem is, lately I haven't been with another woman because all I want is her. Skyla fucking Winters. She's twelve years younger than me, though, and I'm pretty sure that's where the issue lies. I'm an old man to her. She's in her prime.

I finish who the fuck knows how many bottles of beer and put the new empty one on the table. Skyla, having exhausted herself from dancing, leans against me. Being a good friend, I let her. When she yawns and closes her eyes, her hand falls on my dick. I choke down the groan, but instead of continuing to be a good friend and moving her hand, I pull her closer. I'd blame it on the alcohol, but I know it's me.

"So tired…," she mumbles into my chest.

I kiss the top of her head. "We should get you home."

She nods. "Good idea." She hiccups.

I hug her a little closer, but it's the hiccup that snaps me out of my own lust induced haze. I let my other hand trail down her arm until it reaches her wrist. I bring her hand to my lips and kiss it as I stand and pull her up with me.

Wrapping my arm around her waist, I lead her towards Alex and Raleigh so we can say our goodbyes. They'll be leaving for their honeymoon soon anyway.

I pat Alex on the back and side hug him. "We're taking off, man. She's exhausted."

Alex grins and returns the hug. "Thanks for being here." He lets go of me and hugs Skyla.

I hug Raleigh and kiss her on top of the head. "Wouldn't have missed it."

Raleigh stands on her tiptoes and kisses me on the cheek. "My feet hurt so much."

I smile. "I told you not to wear heels."

She rolls her eyes. "I'm surrounded by tall men. I had to do something to offset it."

I laugh. "Enjoy your honeymoon."

I put my arm back around Skyla and lead her outside. I had no intention of driving because I knew having Skyla in close proximity to me during something like this would send me straight to the bottle. I have a driver tonight.

"Ready to head out, Mr. Michaels?" one of our family guards, and my driver, asks me.

"Yeah," I tell him as he opens the door of one of our many black SUVs. I help Skyla into the back and slide in next to her. The guard closes the door and makes his way to the driver's seat. He takes off as I drop my head against the headrest and close my eyes.

Skyla messes me up more than I care to admit to anyone, myself especially. It's not just that I've been relegated to the friend corner. It's that she's very hot and cold with me. We've been in some very heavy makeout sessions at both her house and mine, even in my office at the department. But Skyla always pulls back. She calls me when she's upset, and it always ends with me walking out with blue balls after she kisses me senseless.

I give just as good as I get, but I'd never make her do anything she doesn't want to. As soon as she pushes me away, that's it. It's all in her court. I might get frustrated as fuck, but that's where it ends. I'd never take it out on her.

I know why she does it. I may not like it, but I understand. She has very strong feelings for me. I can see them swimming in her eyes every time she looks at me. She's scared, though. Having feelings and getting close to people means one thing and one thing only.

A relationship like the one she barely escaped with her life.

So, she'd rather keep me at a distance safe for her. Friends. She trusts me to let her take it all at the pace she sets. I'm a very patient man, but three years is a lot of time. A lot of time with the up and down. Me thinking she's about to finally move past the barrier she's set up only for those barriers to slam right back in my face. It's a never ending and vicious circle. She'll go on a date, not like the guy, complain about it all to me, ask to come over or for me to meet at her penthouse, and have it all end with me frustrated and her retreating behind her walls.

I'm not surprised at all at this point when we arrive at her penthouse, and I have her against the wall next to her door with my tongue down her throat. I groan at the taste of whatever expensive wine Alex provided that she was drinking tonight.

"Oh my God, Dane…," she moans. Her leg hooks around mine, effectively hitching her dress up her thighs and giving me easy access to all of her.

"Fuck, baby." I nip her lip and pin her between me and the wall. I grip her barely covered ass and lift her. Her legs wrap around my waist, and I grind myself into her as I kiss her far more deeply.

I let my tongue tangle with hers. Nothing has ever awakened me like she does. Just being around her has me buzzing, but when she lets me kiss her like this, it's the best feeling in the world. Not because of how I feel or how she feels against me. It's because I know she's just as into it as me. I know she wants me as much as I do her. I never want it to end.

Of course, it inevitably does. I sense her pulling away before I even feel her hands on my chest. Why it hurts more this time than any other time is something I'll never be able to explain. Maybe because every time it happens, it gets harder and harder to come back from.

"I can't…," she whispers, her eyes on her hands. Her breath is shuttering as I try to catch mine.

"Skyla, I'm going out of my mind. We're running around in circles. You need to decide what we are because every time this fucking happens, you break me more. There's only so much rejection my heart can take."

"I'm so sorry…" She sniffles.

I let her down and shake my head. "I can't do this anymore. My head is fucking swimming because of you, your taste, and the alcohol." I run my hands through my hair and step back. Her sweet scent and the smell of her arousal is killing me. "I don't even know how the fuck we got here, but it's all or nothing, Skyla. This isn't fair to either of us. I know this is all because of your ex, but this can't keep happening. You need to decide what you want from me. Are we friends or lovers? There's no more in between for me."

The words I've wanted to say for so long fall from my lips, and I can't stop them, even though I see each one cuts her a little deeper.

"You're right, Dane," she says softly. Her tear-filled blue eyes meet mine, and my heart feels like it literally cracks. Her lip quivers. "You don't deserve this." She shakes her head. "You don't deserve anything I'm putting you through." She looks down and turns towards her door.

I want to reach out for her. I want to step closer. I want to hug her. Kiss her. Run my fingers through her silky hair. Anything to make her feel better.

I don't. I stay rooted to my spot like I'm standing in dried cement as she closes the door behind her. It's only when I hear the lock slide into place that I move. I lean my head against her door and let out a long breath.

My fists are over my head against the frame, but I don't let myself beat on it. Instead, I flex my arms until my muscles are shaking. When I feel like I'm not going to lose complete control, I take another deep breath and let it out slowly. I take a step back and stare at her door for a few moments as the war inside rages.

Before I can change my mind, I turn around and slowly walk away.

This time, though, will be the last.

Chapter Two

ᛏ Skyla ᛏ

It's dark.

Quiet.

Too quiet.

If I listen closely enough, I'm sure I could hear a fly breathe, but it doesn't matter. I won't move. I know better than that. Waking him would be disastrous. Dire consequences I'm not sure I could survive. I've gotten through a lot with him. I don't think it would be possible for me to get out of it this time with my life.

He moves.

I hold my breath.

When he groans, I squeeze my eyes shut and hug myself a little bit tighter. I'm on my side facing him. I don't dare turn my back to him. Who knows what he'd do to me. I doubt I could stop him, but at least I'd have a warning. A chance to fight.

"Fuck. I feel like I fought Tyson."

I almost scoff, but I don't. I'm the one with the busted lip, bruised cheek, and handprints all over my body. I'm the one who dares not make any sudden movements. I'm the one who can barely take a breath without feeling like my lungs are going to collapse.

And I'm the one who has to walk into work tomorrow and act like everything is just fine. I'm the one who needs to dress to cover everything and put my makeup on meticulously to hide what he did to me. I'll be the one avoiding questions and making up excuses.

He has no idea what it feels like to lie here frozen with his eyes wide open. Afraid that any movement will wake the monster. He doesn't have a clue what that's like. The toll it takes when the person he loves so much is the one with the power to destroy him.

No.

He doesn't know what that's like. Not as I do.

"Fuck," he groans again as he gets up.

I watch as he goes into the bathroom and closes the door. I know he won't be long, but it's my only chance to get out of here. I know I can't get to my clothes. He'll hear me. I grab the white, button down shirt he tossed onto the armchair in his bedroom. He lives in the penthouse on the top floor of his New York office building.

I'm the Chief Financial Officer at T-Rac Merc. He's the Chief Executive Officer. I know as well as he does that I got the job because he thought I was hot. I worked my way from Junior Accountant to leading my own team. I applied for the CFO position with very little experience and a lot of encouragement from that team. I know my skills, but it wasn't my skills that got me where I am.

It was him.

He might have liked the way I look, but I fell hard for him. For me, it was love at first sight. He was charming, sweet, sexy, smart, and knew all the right things to do and say.

It was when he had me under his spell that it all changed. That's when the control started, and I took it for the dominance I crave. It was never that. It was abuse. I see that now. Him talking down to me wasn't him being dominant. It was him breaking me down.

I button the shirt as I flee from the bedroom as silently as I can. My purse is by the door along with my shoes. If I can get to them, I can get out of here. I just need to get to Austin, my brother. I know he'll help me. I haven't been allowed to see him in so long. We only get to talk while at work.

I quickly grab my purse and shoes. I'm wearing nothing under the shirt, and I hope it's long enough to hide that fact. I'm not allowed to sleep with clothes on. It gives him easier access to me when he wants something. I'm nothing but a fuck toy to him that he can toss around as he sees fit.

I close the door as quietly as possible behind me and start running. I won't take the elevator that opens up right into the penthouse. It's too easy to get trapped in it and stopped by his security when I get to the bottom floor. Instead, I run for the stairs. I don't put my shoes on until I'm nearing the bottom of all fifty flights. There's a back entrance I plan to slip out. It avoids being caught by his security. They have their orders, and they come from him.

I quickly burst through the door as I take out my phone. My plan is to run as far as I can before calling Austin. The further I am away from here, the better.

I realize my mistake too late.

As soon as I open the door, two of his security guards are standing right there with their arms folded across their chests and scowls plastered on their faces.

"Ms. Winters," one of them growls so dangerously that I back away.

"H... hi...," I stammer. "I... j-just... n-needed... a-air."

"There's a perfectly good balcony upstairs, ma'am," the other says. They both loom closer.

My vision darkens. I look for any escape. They're both too big for me to get around. They're blocking the door. If I can get by them, I might have a chance, but I know I don't have a prayer of dodging them. I need a new plan.

Barely thinking it through because I have little choice, I turn and run towards the door that enters the lobby. I'm expecting guards to be on the other side this time, so I know I can duck through them. I'm a small woman. I can use that to my advantage.

As I'm opening the door, I'm already ducking and calling Austin. If he can get here quickly, I might have a chance of outrunning all of them as soon as I can get out of this building. If I don't, then at least he's alerted and can get help.

"Stop her!" one of his guards bark as I duck and dodge between them, battling my way to the door.

Then, I see him.

My eyes widen. "N-no…"

I try to skid to a halt, but it's far too late. His forearm comes out and connects with my throat in a clothesline any WWE Superstar would envy. I have no time to stop myself from crashing to the ground in a heap. I gasp for air and stare up at him wide-eyed. My hand immediately goes to my throat. I know without having a medical degree that he crushed my windpipe, and he'll do nothing to help me.

He doesn't kneel next to me. He stands over me with his guards. "I told you. You're mine. No one else can have you. If I can't have you, then there's only one way to make sure no one else does." He ends with a low, threatening growl.

He's right. He did say that.

And as I try in vain to suck in oxygen, I realize he's made good on his warning.

He killed me.

ೆೆೆ

I wake up screaming and gasping for breath as I claw at the sheets underneath and wrapped around me. Something is around my neck choking me. I know it's not his hands. There's no one else in this room with me. As soon as I opened my eyes, it was the first thing I checked. I always check that.

So, what is it? What's keeping me from getting air into my lungs?

I claw at my neck, continuing to gasp through uncontrollable screaming. I want to stop. I know I'm not in any immediate danger, but my body hasn't caught up to my brain yet. It's a common phenomenon for people with Post Traumatic Stress Disorder. PTSD is a fucked up mess of uncontrollable reactions to situations that appear normal to everyone else.

I finally loosen the sheets from around my throat and throw them off of me as I jump out of the bed. I take gulp after gulp of air as my brain forces my body to listen to it.

Stop screaming! It commands. *Stop it!*

After what seems like an eternity, my voice box finally listens. My lungs expand. My windpipe allows more and more air into my body. My heart eventually slows enough to focus on what it needs to do. Pump that blood through my body. Oxygen begins flowing through my arteries and coming back to my heart through my veins.

For the millionth time during this year since my brother moved in with his girlfriend, I wish he were here. I would give anything to see him storming into my bedroom to ground me from one of my nightmares. He always knows what to do to make me feel safe.

The only other person…

I hold my head and shake it as I breathe. No. I very much fucked everything up with Dane. Again. I have a habit of doing that. It's not like I don't want him. I do. Very much, and not just because I'm sure he could rock my world between my bedsheets. It's because Dane is literally everything I've ever dreamed of in my perfect match. Everything I've wanted; needed and can never have.

I don't deserve him. I'm no good for him. I'm too messed up. Damaged goods. No one wants someone who clings to them in public because they're afraid the Boogeyman will jump out at them. And not just the one in my mind. The one that's real. The one I know lurks in the shadows watching me, even though I never see him. I don't need to. I know he's there. He's always there.

I sit on the edge of my bed and let out a breath as I reach over to flick on the bedside lamp. I know I'm not sleeping anymore. I've only gotten a couple of hours. It's three in the morning, but I know shutting my eyes and being able to get more rest is out of the question.

I push the switch and furrow my brows when nothing comes on. Seconds later, the dim light near the door of my bedroom goes out. It's a sign that the power in the building went out. The backup power comes on instantly. There could be danger. It instantly spurs me into action.

There are rules in situations like this. The first is to not leave my bedroom. It's the safest place. The second is to complete the lockdown process. The rest of the building and my penthouse are inaccessible to anyone without a specific code and several other forms of security. The only thing for me to do is close my shades if they are open. The window is bulletproof, but it's still not wise for people to know exactly where I am.

I hurry to the window and hit the red button. The button I'm only supposed to push in the event of a lockdown. It closes my shades and brings a titanium shield down over my window. I push it just as I catch a glance of a helicopter hovering near my window.

The pilot.

I will never forget those eyes.

Those cold, calculating, burning ember eyes.

Just as the titanium moves into my line of sight safely locking me into the security of my room, he smiles. Just a small one. Barely perceptible.

But I saw it. I saw it all.

I'm supposed to feel secure. I don't.

I scramble away from the window and grab my cellphone and a blanket as I run to the bathroom. I close the door and lock it. I use the light from the phone to guide my way to the bathtub. It's a jacuzzi tub. I love the baths I get to take. They're luxurious and relaxing. I wish I could be taking a bath right now, but I'm not. Instead, I wrap myself in the blanket, hunker down, and hide.

But I'm not completely paralyzed in fear. I call the only person I can think of right now. The only man whose face can chase away the hellhound haunting me.

Dane Michaels.

Tall. Dashingly handsome, yet rugged and rough. Beautiful jade eyes that darken whenever he looks at me. Muscles that could put any gym rat to shame. Dane is perfect.

Safe.

My safe.

"What, Skyla?" he rumbles into the phone. I'm sure I've woken him.

"He's here," I whisper. I don't know that I have to, but I need him. I need him to make me feel safe.

"Who?" he growls low.

"Thurston."

Thurston Maxwell. CEO of T-Rac Merc.

And my controlling, abusive ex-boyfriend. The one I barely escaped with my life from.

"Call your security."

"The power's out," I whisper. "They're on the way, I'm sure, but... I..." I take a deep breath and close my eyes. "I'd feel more comfortable with you here."

There's a long pause. If there was a clock with hands in this bathroom, I'd be hearing it tick the minutes away.

Tick-tock…

Tick-tock…

Tick…

Tock…

"Call your security, Sky…," Dane says damn near a whisper. "I can't be there this time."

I swallow. Hard. "Wh-what..?" My heart beats so fast that it feels like it completely stops.

"You have the best security in the world, Skyla." Dane clears his throat. "They're paid to make you feel safe. I can't do that anymore. I can't be that for you anymore. I won't survive it."

I see nothing in front of me but black static. "Dane… You… can't possibly mean that…" It's my turn to whisper.

"The last three years you've put me through the ringer. I just can't deal with it anymore. One second, you're wanting everything I do. Everything you know I want with you. I've never been dishonest or hidden it. You know how I feel about you. I always said I'd take it at your pace, but when you're practically fucking me one second only to pull back the next… Fuck, Skyla. I can't do this anymore. You say you're protecting your heart, but it's time I protected my own. We're either more than friends or we're not. Or we're just friends or we're not. I can't be on this playing field where I'm always balancing on the fifty-yard line. I can't be shoved past it or lose the yardage I've gained all the time. It's not fucking fair to you or me."

He's right. He's so right. I know he is.

I start to hyperventilate. "Dane, please… Don't… Please don't walk away from me."

"You need to decide what we are. Because this isn't fair to me. You have security there. I'll contact them. Make sure they're guarding you and going through protocols. I'm sure they've already called our contacts in the PD. They've left me a message already. I'll send Cole."

"Please don't -" I'm cut off by rustling before the line very obviously goes silent. Tears sting my eyes. "Please don't give up on me," I whisper.

But it's too late.

I've played with him for far too long. I've let my fears get in the way. Now, I've lost the one person in my life who never failed to make me feel like a Queen. The person who spent so much time building me up and helping me gain the confidence I lost.

I'm the one who messed up.

I'm the one who pushed and pulled him until he finally broke.

I lost him.

Chapter Three

☙ Dane ☙

I drop my phone next to me as I roll on my back and rub my head. I close my eyes, letting out a low growl. Alex and Raleigh flew out for their honeymoon just after their reception last night. I'd just gotten home by the time they were boarding the plane.

I haven't slept a wink. All I can see is Skyla's blue eyes. The lust swimming in them when I had her against the wall.

Not all lust. I saw the feelings. I saw the exact moment those feelings melded with her fears and the second fear took over.

I rub my hands over my face and sit up as I answer my ringing phone. I glance briefly at the caller ID and am relieved it's not Skyla's name that comes up. Relieved even though my heart is fucking broken. I hate what I just did, but I know it's the best option for us both. I can't be back and forth between friends and whatever the fuck else I am to her. Three years is too much of the hot and cold bullshit.

"What?" I growl into my phone.

"You want me to pick you up, Lieutenant?" Cole Westwood, the Sergeant on my taskforce and one of my best friends, asks me.

"No. Take care of it."

There's a bit of a pause before Cole sighs. "What happened?"

"Nothing, Cole. Just take care of it."

"You know I'm calling bullshit, Dane. This has to do with your girl. Why aren't you jumping in your truck and speeding to Lucinio Tech?"

I get out of bed knowing I'm not going back to sleep. "Stop it, Westwood."

"Not a chance. I'm outside."

"Fuck. Let it go, man. Please. I'm fucked up over it enough."

"Then get some jeans on and get your ass out here. This is above my paygrade anyway. There's talk of a fucking chopper caught hovering around the penthouse and the executive suite."

That peaks my interest. "What?" I hold my phone between my shoulder and ear as I throw a pair of jeans on. Cole isn't going away. I know the fucker better than that.

"Yeah. Hovering there. Had a headlight shining into Alex's window before he moved to Skyla's. Circled around and started searching each window of the penthouse."

My heart rate slows a little as I walk to my closet with my jeans still unbuttoned. "Sounds like they were looking for Skyla. Not Alex."

"You want to bet your brother's life on that?"

I sigh as I grudgingly grab a navy blue button down shirt. "Fucking asshole. You know just where to hit."

"Get your ass out here. You can tell me about Skyla on the way. Josh is already heading out with Gavin, Damon, and Lance."

I sigh again and hang up the phone. I put it in my back pocket and finish getting dressed. I button my pants and grab my gunbelt. I throw it on before grabbing my gun and holstering it. If Josh is getting his second and third in command as well as his tech guy, it means he either learned some information, or he's sensing something big is going on. I've learned well over the years to trust the fearless King of Lucinio Mafia, but mostly to trust my brother.

I jog down the stairs of my dark house and straight to the front door. I've always been able to see well in the dark, but it helps when I'm used to where things are. I could close my eyes and still know exactly where everything is in my house. Things in this house are meticulously placed. If anything is moved and not put back, I'll know. People call it obsessive, but it's not. I don't walk behind people when they visit and start putting things back where I had them. But if something is moved, like my couch, by less than a quarter of an inch, I'll know. I call it detail-oriented. Something I need with my job.

After getting my shoes on and locking up my house, I head out to Cole's truck and jump in. I chuckle a little because Cole fucking loves this truck. As soon as he saw it, he had to buy it. Walked right in and paid in cash. Black on black Ford F-150 Raptor. I couldn't help but laugh because we were just leaving a damn interview with a witness to a crime when he spotted it. Brand spanking new. Drove it right off the lot. The leather seats might be my favorite.

"Man. I don't think I'll ever get sick of this truck."

Cole chuckles. "Then buy one. Ain't like you can't afford it. Josh pays you enough."

I grin. "Hell, Ryan paid me enough. How do you think I was able to retire my dad and give him a comfortable life?"

"Time to splurge, old man."

I laugh and backhand him on the arm. "I'm fucking ten years older than you, asshole."

Cole grins. "Big difference between thirty-five and forty-five."

"Do yourself a favor and shut your mouth, kid." I grin, grateful for the teasing, but realize my mistake as soon as the words leave my mouth. I groan. "Don't." The grin falls from my face. He's using my lightened mood as an excuse to bring *her* up.

"Too late." He drives out of the gate to our compound. We both wave at the guards on the way by. "What's going on with Skyla?"

I sigh and rub my head. "You're not letting it go, are you?"

"I'm definitely not. Everything seemed fine last night."

"Well, things change." I turn and look out the window.

"Did she fuck you, then tell you to leave?"

I roll my eyes. "Fuck, Cole."

"So she did. And it pissed you off."

I turn and glare at him. "Dammit, Cole. It wasn't that, okay? I'm just fucking tired of the hot and cold game. One second we're all over each other. The next, she's breaking my heart by pushing me away. She goes out with another guy and calls me to rescue her if she doesn't like him. Or calls me over after she says goodnight to him. I haven't been dishonest with her. She knows how I feel. I know how she feels. I know she's scared.

But I can't bust through it. Three years trying. Last night was one too many times. It cut a lot deeper. It cuts deeper every damn time."

Cole is quiet. He calmly keeps his eyes on the road. I'm not sure if I want to hit the dashboard or him. My too fucking composed demeanor wins out, and I do neither. Instead, I heave in a deep breath as I hit the button for the window. As it goes down, a cool Chicago breeze hits my face.

"You know it's because of what she went through," Cole finally says after several moments.

"Yeah."

He stops in front of Lucinio Tech and puts a hand on my arm to stop me from escaping like I want to. "Look, man. I fucking get it. I'm not even going to tell you to work it out because I know how badly that hurts. What I will say is that she needs you right now." He nods towards the building. "Whatever the hell is happening right now had to have terrified her because she's the one who asked her security team to call Josh."

I shake my head and close my eyes with a groan. "Fuck this headache. And fuck my pride. I should've listened to her instead of telling her to go to her team. She was probably scared to death her team was betraying her and went to the one person she felt she could trust."

Cole lets go of my arm. "Doesn't matter now, Lieutenant. She needs help. I still don't know much more from what Josh said, but I do know that she's scared."

We both step out of the truck. I'm immediately drowning in thoughts of her. My emotions are at war with each other. I want to run to her; hug her. At the same time, I want to sprint back to the truck instead of walking into the building behind Cole. I want to leave him here and speed home because I know if I see her, that's going to be it. I won't be able to walk away again.

We step into the elevator, and my heart starts racing faster and faster with each floor we pass. By the time the doors open on her floor, I'm fighting myself to breathe normally and not start hyperventilating. I should win a damn award. I'm falling apart inside, but there's not a soul who would look at me and have any fucking clue.

"Lance is already on surveillance. He's got Skyla with him. She kept saying the person in the chopper was him. Wouldn't say who," Josh, already in mafia boss mode, says as soon as we reach him. "I need you and

Cole in the room looking for anything out of place. Her security said someone breached her door last night before she was home. Surveillance shows nothing, though, and I don't have a fucking clue how they'd know that."

"Nothing about what you just said sits right with me," I grumble. It means he's thinking exactly what I've already come to the conclusion of. Whether it's an accurate conclusion will be proven or disproven with evidence because that's what I do.

"It shouldn't sit right with you, man," Gavin says. "Nothing about this bullshit is right. I've already put in orders to get her the fuck out of here."

"And I just sent more guards to Alex from Ryan's team just in case we have a leak." Josh pinches the bridge of his nose. "Everything was going so fucking well. I should know better by now."

"Don't beat yourself, bro." I pat him on the back. "The guards on her are Lucinio Tech."

"Not like they don't go through heavy vetting," Cole says. "Especially these two."

"Also doesn't mean they can't get paid off. Everyone likes money. Some people love it and would do anything for it." Josh yawns. "Gav and I will be down with Lance. Damon should have just finished his perimeter check. Fuck, I'm tired."

I nod. "Go check on them. We got this."

Josh nods. He and Gavin head for the elevators. Cole and I enter the already open door. It lets me know that Josh and Gavin have already been in here. I flip the lightswitch on and raise an eyebrow when nothing happens.

"The fuck?" Cole asks, voicing my thoughts perfectly.

I flip the switch off and fold my arms over my chest as I look around. "Other than that, what's the first thing you notice?"

"Backup power is on, but only in here."

"Did they say power went out to the whole building?"

"Yes, sir. It definitely did."

"Then why is she still on backup power?"

"Good question. We'll have to find out."

We both start combing the room. I've been doing this a long time. I know where most people hide bugs or hidden cameras. But I've also been working a long time with the mafia. I know that a lot of these guys are smart. When someone is working with the mafia or highly trained, they don't pick typical places. Not under a table or chair. Not behind a plant.

No.

These fuckers are going to get creative. I smile when I see Cole looking behind picture frames and in cupboards. I've taught him very well. I know Josh will have someone in here with a detector for bugs, but we'll find them all first.

I head for the bedroom and check the usual places, but I also check the bedframe. Sure as shit, I find one near the frame. I remove it with a chuckle and circle the room. I find a small, almost undetectable camera on the end of the curtain rod. I find a couple more bugs hidden throughout her room, but my favorite is the camera that's hidden discreetly in a vase of flowers.

I find a couple more cameras in her bathroom, one positioned at her shower, the other at the toilet, and another bug on top of her medicine cabinet. I nearly lose it because each of these cameras would see her in her most intimate moments. The ones in her bedroom would see everything she does, including sleeping and getting dressed or undressed.

Cole and I search the rest of the penthouse. We each individually search places the other already has just so we don't miss anything. By the time we're done, it's almost seven in the morning. Skyla's emergency activation is still in place, so the apartment is only lit by the backup power. We can't see outside, but I know the sun is probably lighting the sky in brilliant colors that I certainly don't feel.

"Motherfucker had this whole place covered," Cole growls when we meet in the middle of the living room. One of Lance's tech guys has shown up to run his equipment through. "Even had a camera in the dollhouse on top of the mantle."

He nods to a dollhouse I helped Skyla build on her birthday two years ago. It was a replica of one she had as a child and kept into adulthood. Her father built it, and she cherished it her entire life. She left all of her possessions at her ex's when she left. That was one of them, but it was in pieces. Her ex destroyed it the night before and made her watch just before he beat her to within an inch of her life.

"Cameras and audio all throughout her room. He could see everything she did. Sleep. Dress. Undress. Shower. Go to the bathroom."

Cole shakes his head as we both trail slowly behind the tech guy. "How long do you think this was happening?"

"I don't know. Instincts say it just happened. Some of these were in my line of vision. I would've seen them pretty clearly had I been sitting with her on the couch watching a movie. I haven't been in here for about a week. Last night, we stopped outside the door, made out. She pushed me away. I left and told her I couldn't do this anymore. That's why when she called I told her to call her security."

"I get it, man. I can't say I wouldn't have done the same thing. Need to put that shit behind you right now, though. Because no fucking way Josh is letting her stay with her brother and his girl. He'll put guards on them, but he'll make her stay in the compound."

I growl low and glare at the wall. "I know." I also know my brother. He'll make her stay in the compound, for certain. Only he'll take it a step further and make her stay with me. I look at Cole. Maybe I can sweet talk him into taking her.

"No."

I sigh. He knows me too well. "Come on."

"No. Work it out with her. Maybe this will be the best thing."

"You're such a dick."

"I get that a lot. Thank God, I'm well-endowed and can back up the fucking insult. Turn it into a compliment." He gives me a cocky grin.

"No more bugs or cameras Mr. Michaels," the tech guy says.

I nod. "Thanks."

We all leave the penthouse. I close the door behind me and follow both Cole and the tech guy to the elevator. I don't say anything until we reach the bottom floor. We're heading for the security room to check in with Josh. I'm hoping Skyla is locked safely in another room because I need to harden myself again before I face her. Like that one song says, she's the death of peace of mind.

A peace I know I'm never getting back.

Chapter Four

🍎 Skyla 🍎

"Skyla, dammit…," Austin says as he leans back in his chair. He levels me with a glare that I don't need but deserve. "Forget all of that. You need to tell him. You need to tell all of them. You know I will if you don't."

I glare right back at him. "You fucking won't, Austin. I'm nothing but a burden to them. Look at what happened with me living in Alex's building. I've brought my dark past right to his feet."

"You're my sister, and I love the hell out of you, but this isn't standing with me. You're telling them, or I am. It's as simple as that."

"You can't force me to talk."

"Nope. And you can't force me to not talk. I've kept the major shit quiet at your request. I've let you tell them what you've wanted to. I let you confirm things they found out that you didn't want them to know. Time that you come completely clean."

I sigh in frustration. "They know what they need to."

"Not nearly enough, Skyla! Fuck! It's not just me you're putting in danger this time!" He runs his fingers through his hair, and I finally lose it.

The tears I've been fighting for hours finally spill over as I stand. "That isn't fair, and you know it!"

Austin stands just as angrily. "Isn't it?" he yells right back at me. "What about Rosie and Dallas? What about the Lucinio family, huh? All of them!"

Austin is tall. He towers over me, but I've never feared my brother. I stand toe to toe with him and push him back a step. "That's not fair! Their safety isn't my responsibility!"

He steps right back to me, though, and keeps yelling at me. "It's not? What about the kids, huh? What about Harper and Jordan? What about Tait, Chris, and Jackson? You bringing danger right to their doorstep isn't putting them in danger? That's not on you?" His eyes darken enough to make me swallow.

"Back off, Austin!" I push him again, but he doesn't move this time.

"Hey! Enough!"

My heart leaps a mile at the sound of the deep and commanding voice suddenly filling the room even more than his dominating presence does. With very little effort, Dane has me and Austin separated and has taken complete control of the situation.

Austin's glare doesn't lessen. "You're telling him right now, or I am," he growls.

"Telling me what?" Dane asks. I haven't looked up at him, but I know his eyes are fixed on me. I can feel them just as I can feel myself breathing. They're just as hard as the sharp breaths I'm forcing into my lungs.

I close my eyes and shake my head as I swipe at the tears rolling down my cheeks. "I'll deal with it myself. I always have."

Austin scoffs. "And look where that got you, Skyla. Right back in Thurston's arms."

"Someone needs to start talking," another deep voice says. My head snaps to the tall man leaning against the doorframe with jeans and a black t-shirt on. His muscular arms are folded across his chest, and his ankles are crossed.

Josh Lucinio.

And he doesn't look like he's in the mood to deal with any bullshit. Especially from me. His blue eyes are darkened and look almost coal black. I don't blame him. I can't imagine he liked being woken up so early with a threat to his brother. For all he knows, the chopper circling Lucinio Tech wasn't for me. It was for Alex.

"Take Austin out for a coffee," Josh commands. Like Dane's, his eyes don't leave me.

"You got it," Dane says. I don't miss the relief in his voice.

I wouldn't blame him even if I could. I know I hurt him. His face when he left, those slumped shoulders and dead eyes, gave him away. I killed him inside with just a few words, and I deserved everything he said to me on the phone. I deserve to be pushed away. My heart breaking all over again as I watch him walk away from me for the second time is something I definitely earned.

"Sit down," Josh orders as he comes fully into the room and closes the door. I obey and drop in a chair. I'm too tired to argue, but I wouldn't anyway. I thrive off commands and order. Chaos makes me anxious. I need the dominance. "Tell me what the fuck is happening, Skyla." Josh sits in a chair across from me facing the door. He'll never allow himself to be put into a position where he can't see a threat coming. "Fill in the blanks."

I let out a breath and drop my head on my arms resting on the table. "This is hard, Josh. It's been buried for a long time. If I tell you, it all comes to the surface again and puts so many people in so much danger."

"I can handle it, Skyla. I command a goddamn army. And if I asked, I could literally command the fucking United States military. Hell. I already have. So, talk. Tell me what's so buried that not even my hacker can find it."

I groan before slowly lifting my head. I don't have the strength to do anything more than rest it on my arms though as I look at him. "Thurston Maxwell. You know who he is."

"Unfortunately."

I close my eyes. "You know my relationship with him was volatile."

"I don't know that I'd use that word. He beat the fuck out of you numerous times. Abusive is better terminology."

I sniffle and nod my head a little bit in agreement. He's right. It was violent. "I didn't just escape."

Josh puts his arms on the table as he leans forward. He looks calm and collected, but I know him. He's ready for a fight. Thankfully, not with me. Josh is capable of world destruction. I wouldn't want to be in the path of that.

"I knew if I left, he'd find me. I spent a lot of money to keep that from happening."

"You paid a member of the Crane Mafia to hide you."

My lips part slightly. I quickly sit up as my eyes meet his. "H-how did you know that?"

"The security firm you hired to get you and Austin out is one of Ryan Crane's businesses. After we got you out of the shitty neighborhood you were in, the firm you hired to keep an eye out for you and your brother went to Ryan because you'd gone missing, and one of their guys was found dead."

I put my head down. I knew he was found. It's a guilt I've lived with for the past three years. He was killed because of me. I've always known Thurston did it. "I didn't know there was an affiliation," I whisper. I lift my heavy head once more. "Why didn't you say anything?"

"Because it didn't matter. I got the information I needed. I shared it with my leadership and with Ryan. Everything else was up to you. I made sure Dane knew what he needed to, but I wasn't going to tell him everything, Skyla. That was never my decision to make or my information to give. He knows pertinent things to keep you safe. He didn't need to know that you hired someone to get you out. At least not from me. That was always something you should've shared with him."

I sigh as I stand and hug myself. "I know. Okay?" I say the words quietly as I turn my back on him. I walk slowly to the wall and turn towards him again as I lean against it. I'm so tired that if I don't stand, I'm going to pass out. I'm sure of it.

"So, fill in the blanks, Skyla. I have what their records say, but you weren't exactly forthcoming with them either. There's a lot of missing links."

I shrug. "Because there's nothing to say. I was scared. He threatened me. He threatened Austin. It was always about protecting Austin. That's why I kept going back and enduring it for as long as I did. It was because of my brother. I didn't want anything to happen to him. Thurston is a powerful man. Cruel. I didn't doubt for a second that he'd kill Austin. I'd rather he killed me instead and left him alone."

"Come on, Skyla. You know me a lot better than that. Three years. You've been here for three years. Why Chicago of all places? Was it just because of the job? Or was there another reason?"

His question is like a sucker punch right to my chest. I do know him better than that. I know he's smart. I know he never asks questions he doesn't already know the answer to. And if he doesn't know, he definitely has an inclination of the answer. And he'll never let the subject drop until he has all of the information he wants. He has ways of getting information out of people, both violently and non-violently. While I don't fear him in the slightest, he's just as much a brother to me as Austin is by this point. I'm very close with the Lucinio family. Josh knows what he's doing.

"Austin did get recruited. So did I. The company did go under before we really even started. So, we did end up in a shitty part of town because we didn't have a lot of income. Hiring the security firm to help us was expensive. It took all of my savings and Austin's, but I'm not stupid. I know we got a heavy discount. We couldn't afford them if we didn't. They even offered to put us up somewhere, but we both refused because we believed with them around, everything would be okay. We didn't think it would take so long to get jobs. In retrospect, it really didn't."

"Okay. So, why Chicago? They gave you a choice. They had a corporate office in London. That's much further away than Chicago."

"You're right. It is. It's also where T-Rac Merc has their overseas headquarter offices. We both felt like we'd be putting ourselves right into Thurston's hands by going there. He doesn't have offices in Chicago. He doesn't like Chicago. He thinks the city is crime ridden and beneath him and his worth. Third-class citizens, and even worse than them. If this were the Titanic, Chicago would be the boiler rooms. We chose here because of that. And... well, because of you. Because of the Crane Mafia."

"Why?"

"We did our research, Josh. We didn't come here with the intention of..." I trail off and sweep my arm over the room. "The intention wasn't to end up working here at Lucinio Tech and becoming close to you and your family. Lucino Tech having the jobs posted was so lucky for us. Getting hired was even more lucky. We knew exactly who Alex was, though. We applied because we needed the jobs and Alex was hiring, thankfully, for exactly what we were looking for. Call it divine intervention if you want to, but it was truly like fate had intervened.

Especially when we were put up in the penthouse. The security in this building is second to none. But we chose here because we knew you were here. We knew your reputation. We knew if we needed help, we could count on you and your family. To him, Chicago is crime ridden and rat infested. To us, this is the safest place in the world because of you and the Crane's."

Josh cracks a barely there smile, but I see it. "Okay. Tell me what the fuck made you run and hire bodyguards."

I shrug a little. "Isn't it obvious?"

"Enlighten me." He leans back in his chair and folds his arms across his chest again. I truly believe it's his signature style.

"He almost killed me. I know that was in the reports. I had to divulge that. I barely got out with my life. Austin met me in front of the building. Thurston shot at us. We couldn't go to Austin's apartment. They'd know to go there. We knew they'd figure out a way to track his car. Thurston is an abusive asshole, but he's not stupid. So, we borrowed a car, meaning stole. We stole it. We got rid of our phones. We got new ones. Paid in cash. We found the security company and drove straight there."

"There's no record of you at any hospital after this."

I shake my head. "Nope. I never went. Because I knew he would be looking there. The security company found me a private doctor to check me over. I stayed with Austin above their building. When we finally felt safe enough to start applying for jobs, with the firm's encouragement, we started to question if we should get new identities. We didn't because we were told we wouldn't need to. Not with our security. And for a while, they were right. We weren't being bothered."

"That didn't last, though."

I shake my head again as I tiredly sit down. I rub the grit from my eyes and fight back a yawn. That never works, though, and I yawn anyway. "No. It didn't. I've felt him. I've seen him in shadows. I thought I was being paranoid. I have PTSD from what he did to me. I wake up screaming from night terrors. I get shivers if I'm alone because I feel like I'm being watched. It took me a long time to realize that I really was being watched. It's the reason I asked Alex for more security. After the guard on me had been killed, I ended my contract with the firm. I didn't want more trouble for them. I didn't want them to lose anyone else."

"They know the risks they take."

"Yeah. That didn't make it easier for me. He was killed because of me. That will always be something I struggle with. I didn't know the firm was under Ryan's leadership or that he owned it or whatever, but that wouldn't have changed anything. His life was taken because of me."

"That's still not all, Skyla. You asked Alex for security. He got me involved. I get that it's because you fear Thurston. I get the reasons. I even understand that part of what goes into this is that he's got a lot of money and is quite powerful in your eyes. He can do whatever he wants. He's a millionaire. What I don't get, though, is why hide all of this? If you've felt him or seen him previously, why not tell me? Why not tell Dane or Alex? Fuck, even one of the girls. You've gotten close to them. Why not tell someone that you feel like he's been around? Why let it get to this point?"

"Because, Josh. Telling you puts you in danger. My security was aware that I felt unsafe at times. I even asked Alex if he could put someone on Austin, and he did."

"Skyla, come on." Josh stands with a sigh and reaches out a hand for mine as he stops next to me. I take it, and he pulls me up. "I'm a fucking mafia boss. There's no way in all of creation he can come close to taking me out. I have way too many people who have my back." He leads me to the door and opens it.

"That's really not the point."

"You're afraid that he's going to get to me or Alex or someone else. That he's going to hurt someone you love to get to you." Josh leads me out. "So, this is what we're going to do. You're not staying here because I know there's something you're not telling me."

"My head of security works for Thurston!" I blurt out.

Josh stops and spins on me so quickly, I nearly run right into his chest. "What?"

"I don't know. I suspect. I heard him on the phone last night after Dane left. He came over and did his usual sweep through the penthouse. He was on the phone. He was talking quietly. I heard him say Alex was gone and Dane left. He passed it off that he was talking to his partner, but just hours later, we go into emergency lockdown, and I literally see Thurston hovering outside my bedroom window staring right at me. And that's not all. They took forever to get in here. And when they did, the other person on my detail said that they would have been here sooner but couldn't get in. I asked how that was possible, and he said that his partner lost his access key."

Josh raises an eyebrow. "There is no access key."

I nod. "That's what I said. And when I confronted the head of my detail about it, he said that security had changed. They had an access key now. He even made a show of going back to his room to look. He was super pissed that his partner had entered the room without him and already had me packing up to leave, per protocol, until they could figure out what was happening."

Josh squeezes my hand as he rubs his head. "Fuck, Zekeih is going to be just as pissed as I am."

"I wasn't even allowed to call Zekeih. I don't even have my phone. It was taken. He said it was per protocol, but it's not."

"Protocol is you calling Zekeih," Dane rumbles from behind Josh. I hadn't even seen that he and Austin had come back. I must be more tired than I thought.

My eyes automatically snap to Dane as I nod. My lip trembles because all I want to do is hug him, but I know how badly I fucked that up. That saying is really true. A person never knows what they have until they don't have it anymore.

I took total advantage of him, and now I've lost him.

With each breath I take, that knowledge seeps deeper into my core and breaks me a little more until all I am is a bunch of shattered pieces scattering in the Chicago wind.

Chapter Five

🍎 Dane 🍎

"Take Skyla to your place. Get Austin and his girl into the guest house." Josh's command makes me involuntarily growl.

"She can stay with Austin. The guest house is -"

Josh narrows his eyes as he cuts me off. "Not a question. She stays with you."

I typically wouldn't back down to anyone. It's not in my DNA, but I'll back down to him. I close my mouth and shake my head. It's not because I'm afraid of him. It's because I trust him. Whatever his reasons are for what he just said is happening is enough for me.

Doesn't mean I have to like it, though. "You know you're explaining yourself," I grumble. I take Skyla's hand. "Let's go." I pull her towards the entrance but she tugs her hand out of mine.

"I have nothing with me. I need to grab clothing. I still have to work."

I shoot her a glare. "They'll get your stuff." I flick my eyes towards Josh and Austin. "Now, let's go." I take her hand again and pull her with me, tightening my grip when she tries to pull away again.

"Dane, let me go. I can walk on my own."

"Oh, I know. But you have a tendency to back off at the drop of a dime. Don't need to turn away and you be running down the sidewalk."

"That's no fair," she whispers.

I shrug even though I know the comment was a low blow. "Life ain't fair, sweetheart." I stop near one of our SUVs parked outside the building and open the back door. "In." I turn to her as coldly as I can manage, but her lip trembling just about breaks my resolve.

"I'm sorry, Dane. Really..." She says nothing more as she lowers her head and climbs into the backseat of the SUV. I close the door and use the few seconds it takes me to open the passenger door.

"She doesn't move. She stays right here until I get back," I say to the guard driving.

"Yes, sir," he responds.

Josh always keeps a guard in the driver seat of the SUVs he takes just in case he needs to make a quick escape. Even if he's driving one of his cars or something, he always has guards with him. Some follow. Some lead. Josh is never without them. He's smart. He's a powerful man and always has people gunning for him. Literally. The amount of attempts on his life just since I've known him is an astounding number.

I close the passenger side door and glare into the backseat. Skyla's knees are tucked into her chest and she has her arms wrapped around them. I can tell she's silently crying by the movement of her shoulders. It takes all of me not to open that door and take her in my arms.

My broken heart doesn't allow it, though. I'm pissed I'm hurt at all, but I'm man enough to admit that the reason I feel the way I do is because of how fucking in love with the sexy blond I am.

I push the door to the building back open and almost crash into Austin. He's carrying a duffel bag over his shoulder.

"It's her 'get the fuck out' bag. It has all the stuff she'll need for a few days."

"Thank you, Austin."

"Look, man. It's not my place to tell you what to do, but she's been through a lot. I know she's really only scratched the surface with you, but..." Austin shakes his head. "She's fucking stubborn, but don't give up on her. She loves you. She's happy with you. She just needs to get out of her head." Austin drops his head as he walks out the door. I follow him thinking hard about his words.

I suppose it's really nothing I didn't already know. Skyla has told me a lot about what happened to her. I know why she's so jaded and why those walls she built are so high, but getting through them when she pushes me so far away as often as she does has never been easy.

Not that I don't welcome a challenge, but I'm fucking tired. I'm tired of seeing her give herself to other men, then come running back to me. I run a hand down my face as he climbs in next to Skyla. I slide into the front passenger seat and try to shut out the sounds of her quiet sobbing as Austin hugs her.

"Mr. Lucinio sent a team to Mr. Winters' home. They'll be escorting his security and girlfriend to the guest house in the family compound," the guard says to me.

I nod. "Home sounds like a good plan," I grumble.

I'm so fucking torn. I rub my forehead as I lean back and close my eyes. It should be me comforting her, but I know that as soon as I take her in my arms, I won't be able to back off without it completely breaking me. I'm already fucked up enough over her. I've never felt for anyone like I do her.

But I'm also not an asshole. At least completely. I know I can be. I also know I can't walk away from her. I just need her to decide what the fuck we are because I can't be an in between like this. Good enough for friends, fun enough to make out with, but not good enough to be in a relationship with. I know it's her fear to trust after what she went through, but I still deserve more than what I'm getting. I'm not a damn wolf in search of the little scraps she throws me just to survive.

I growl under my breath as the headache decides to up its level and stab me behind the eye. Probably deserved. I went home and drank a couple more beers before I laid down. Didn't sleep a fucking wink, but I can sure feel the alcohol sloshing through me. Probably one of the two reasons I can't think clearly.

The other is Skyla's subtle scent wrapped around me. It's something fruity and tropical but far from overpowering.

Exactly like her.

I'm fairly certain I fall asleep on the way to the compound because before I know it, I feel a subtle nudge against my arm.

I yawn. "Please say we're home."

"Yes, sir. Just dropped off Mr. Winters. Pulled up to your house now."

"Thanks," I rumble as I get out. Skyla silently follows. I walk to the back to grab her bag that Austin tossed back there after he got in, but she beats me to it and grabs it. I take it from her. "I've got it," I growl.

She looks up at me wide eyed still holding the strap of the duffle bag tightly. "I can -"

"Skyla. Let it go. I have it." I can feel the anger I'm trying to hold back shining in my eyes. She wisely lets go. I close the hatch to the SUV and point to the house. Like a good girl, she scurries for the door. I pinch the bridge of my nose as I follow her. I stop at the driver's side window of the SUV. "Heard anything from Josh?"

"Yes, sir. He's on his way back with Cole. Said get some sleep. He'll talk to you later about the shit they found. He said it's a lot."

I let my hand drop to my side and look up at the sky, bright with the morning sun. After a second I look back down at him. "Thanks, man." I tap the hood as I walk to my door.

Skyla has already entered and shut the door behind her. She's one of the few people who has full security access to this property, including my house. I don't even know why I allowed it to happen. One day, I just felt like she needed it. If she ever needed help, she had a place to go.

When I walk in, Skyla is standing in the middle of the room hugging herself like she's never been here before and doesn't know what to do. It infuriates me because she's been here countless times. She probably knows this house as well as I do.

I growl under my breath for I'm sure the hundredth time tonight. I grip the handles on the bag a little tighter and walk past her without saying a word. She follows just like I expect she will. I take the stairs two at a time, needing to be away from her as quickly as possible. I'm fighting hard between screaming at her to try and make her see what she has in front of her and slamming her against a wall where I can kiss her senseless. Neither option seems like the best one, so as she trudges behind me, I stride down the hall to the guest bedroom that's the furthest from my bedroom.

I take a deep breath when I hear her whimper when she realizes what I'm doing. I open the door to the guest bedroom of my seven bedroom home. This room has its own bathroom. She has everything she needs in here. And if I can be gone to work before she wakes up and not come back until she goes to sleep, all the better.

"Get some sleep," I tell her after setting the bag on the bed. "You need it."

Her arms are still locked around her midsection, and she's looking down. "Yes, sir," she whispers.

In any other case, that would have me solid as a fucking diamond, but I know her well. I know exactly where her head just went.

Him.

Fucking *Thurston Maxwell.*

After everything we've been through, I don't know how the fuck she can possibly think of him when it comes to me. Even if I'm pissed off, she knows I'd never hurt her. So, her standing there hugging herself like she's trying to protect herself and saying 'yes, sir' like it's the only fucking way to placate me sends me to a new level of irritated and shoots me straight to angrily frustrated.

"Come on, Skyla. Really?"

Her eyes snap to mine. I can see the fear. "I -"

"Don't. Don't say a damn word. I'm not him. Fuck, you know I'd never fucking touch you. Not like he did. You know how I feel about you. You're really going to sit there and look at me with fear in your eyes? Give me that fucking 'yes, sir' bullshit like you used to do to him to ease his mind so he didn't hit you? When the hell have I ever made you feel unsafe, Skyla? Huh?"

Her eyes widen, and she shakes her head. My heart both skips a beat and feels like it's being squeezed at the same time. "Dane, it's not like that…"

"Then what? Fucking talk to me!" The words burst out of me. I couldn't control it even if I wanted to. "Do you think I fucking like that I'm good enough to talk to about the guys who don't work out in your life, but that I'm not good enough to be the only man in your life? You think I enjoy watching you go out with others? You think it's easy for me to be good enough to help get their taste off your tongue, but not to be the one who gets to stick around? Because it's not! I fucking hate it!"

"Dane, it's not like that!" Her words fall from her lips just like the tears spill from her eyes. It's the tears that break me, but I'm still angry.

"That's exactly what this is! I'm good enough to be a friend. Good enough to fuck around with. Definitely not good enough to be the one who shows you how a woman should be treated, though, right? As soon as we start making that kind of progress, it's out the fucking door for me, right?"

She shouts in frustration as she stomps her pretty little foot. "Just listen! For five seconds!"

I don't know if it's the fact that she's finally acting like herself and not like a scared little girl around me, or if it's how adorable she looked when she stomped her foot, but I shut my mouth. I fold my arms across my chest and level her with a glare.

She paces the room for a second while she composes herself. While that sexy corporate boss facade slides back into place. If she thinks I'm letting her hide behind it, she has another thing coming. I'm not letting her do it because it's her way of shoving her emotions down.

She takes a deep breath, but my glare must bring that level of calm back down a few notches because I watch as the anger fills her eyes once more. Good. Let her be pissed at me. Maybe we'll get somewhere this way.

"How can you not see it?" she finally asks me. "How can you not see that you're the one man who scares me because of how quickly I can see myself letting my guard down with you?"

I let my arms drop. I can feel my jaw drop in disbelief. "That's what I fucking want! I want you to let your guard down! You don't need to have it up with me! How many times do I have to prove to you that I'm not like him? I'm fucking in love with you!"

I watch all of the tension drain from her shoulders and drop from her clenched fingers. She stares at me in both shock and wonder. I've told her that I like her. I like spending time with her. I've even made it clear that I can see us together.

But not once have I ever told her that I'm in love with her.

I never once uttered those words because I didn't want to scare her. I felt if I did, she'd run. By the look on her face right now, I'm right.

"No... You... can't love me, Dane." She reaches up and wipes her eyes as she turns and runs for the door.

Unfortunately for her, I'm a lot faster. "Skyla, stop." I don't mean for my voice to crack. She doesn't know just how deeply those words cut me.

She sniffles and tries to pull away. "Don't, Dane. I'm not worthy -
"

"Not worthy of what? Love? How can you think that? How
fucking far did he push you for you to honestly believe that you're not
worthy of love?"

The tears are falling faster now. She tries to swipe them away, but
it's useless. "I'm... n-not!" She pulls away from me again. I lose my grip,
and she sprints for the door once more, but I recover quickly.

"Skyla!" I sprint down the hallway after her, catching her just
before she reaches the stairs. "Stop! Skyla, enough!" My voice drops an
octave, reaching a level I don't often use. Her eyes flash as her mouth parts
slightly. "Enough. Fuck, how can you think that? How can you honestly
look at yourself and think you're not worthy? You're fucking smarter than
that. You're beautiful. You're kind and caring. You're the most selfless
person I've ever met in my life. You're so strong. You survived a
relationship with a man who didn't deserve you. A man who showed his
weakness with every fucking blow you took."

Her chest heaves as she shakes her head. The tears don't stop. She
doesn't even try to wipe them away anymore. She looks down at her feet
as her body wracks with sobs. I let my hand fall to hers as I release the grip
on her arm.

"He d-didn't feel w-weak..." She chokes on her words and cries
harder.

I lose every shred of the small grasp of control I have. Wanting
nothing more than to prove to her just how much I truly love her, I run my
fingers through her hair and tug. When she looks up at me, I do my all to
show her through my eyes how worthy she is. How special. Perfect.

I lower my voice once more as I lean down. I stop just before her
pretty lips. "Sky, you're so much stronger than you believe. You got back
up. You got out. You proved every damn day just how much better and
stronger than him you are. You showed him your strength and his
weakness every day, baby. Can't you see that?"

She searches my eyes for so long, I think she might've forgotten
how to speak. "Dane..."

I tangle my fingers in her hair at the nape of her neck. "You're so -
"

She cuts me off, slamming her lips against mine as she wraps her arms around me. I take a step back to steady us both. I drop my hand from her hair and wrap my arms around her. My tongue meets every lash of hers as I lift her up. Her legs wrap around me like it's the most natural thing in the world, and she kisses me deeper. She squeezes her thighs around my waist and tightens her arms around my shoulders.

I'm gone.

I carry her to my bedroom, which is the closest to the stairs, and kick the door shut behind me. "I'm gonna show you how much you mean to me, Skyla. I'm gonna prove to you you're worth it even if it kills me." I kiss down her jaw to her neck and reign myself in. I want nothing more than to plunge inside her pussy, but that's not what this is about. Not this time.

I set her down next to my bed. Shakily, she tries to strip her t-shirt, but I grab her wrists and shake my head. I put her hands above her head and slowly lift her shirt. I let my thumbs glide over her skin as I remove it. As soon as I have it off, I lean down and kiss her once more. Only this time, the kiss is slow. Instead of wrestling with her tongue, I'm gently stroking hers with mine while I remove her silky blue bra and toss it.

She watches me as I kiss her. I hold her close but make no move to push her sleep pants down. Not until she lets her eyes fall closed and I feel her relax. Then, and only then, do I tuck my thumbs into her waistband and push them down.

I kiss a trail from her lips to her neck, then down her collarbone to her nipples. I suck each one of them into my mouth in turn, eliciting a gasp from her. I smile as I look up at her. She's looking at me with such wonder, and I can't help the way my dick reacts to her.

Her hands grip my shoulders. She trembles and shakes her head. "I can't…"

I kiss down her stomach until I reach the crux between her thighs. I look up at her as I finish removing the sleep pants. Silky. Just like her golden skin.

"Okay. Tell me to stop."

It's a simple request, but I know exactly what it does for her. It puts the control in her hands. Control she's very obviously never felt like she's had with anyone. I keep my eyes on her wide blue ones and trail my fingertips up her legs until I reach her hips. I stop as she watches me. She swallows, and her eyes start to shine.

"I…" She trails off.

I shake my head. "No. Words. Tell me to stop. Or tell me to keep going, Skyla. Your choice."

I don't want her to utter the words I feel like she's about to. I want to show her how I feel for her, but if she won't let me do it this way, I'll find other ways.

One thing I know is I'm not leaving this time…

… And I won't let her run.

Chapter Six

ᛏ skyla ᛏ

Usually, my mind is quiet. I have the ability to focus like no other. I can multitask. I'm able to get things done because of those two factors. I don't get distracted. My thoughts don't wander. At least they don't when I'm working. I can't say I don't catch them wandering during times when I'm alone.

Right now, though, Dane has me short circuiting. I'm trembling. Words won't formulate because every thought I've ever had about him and this exact moment are at war with every other thought I have about why this is a terrible idea. How I'm not worth the love of a man like him. I'm a mess. I'm not as composed on the inside as I appear on the outside.

Dane knows all of this. He's seen me at my best and worst. Everything he's said to me is at direct odds with all the things I'm conditioned to believe about myself. I'm stupid and useless. I'm annoying and not pretty. I'm boring and suck in bed. People just put up with me, even though I can't do anything right. Dane, though, he makes me feel smart and worth the air I breathe; worthy of the atmosphere he creates. I'm beautiful and irresistible. I'm fun to be around. I'm everything he's wanted and more.

I've never had any kind of control with Thurston. I was expected to just take whatever he gave me. If I wanted something, I was degraded and told I was demanding. I was slut shamed, even though I'd never been with anyone other than him at that point. I was told to shut up and let him take what he needed. When he was done, I was discarded until he wanted more. Don't talk unless spoken to. Look and act a certain way. That was my life.

Now, here's Dane on his knees in front of me, asking me if it's okay if he touches me. My brain and my heart are screaming yes. I want him to touch me more than I've wanted anything in my life. The rest of my body is paralyzed, though. Usually, my response to him when we get to any point in our fucked up sexual game is to run.

Today, though, I'm frozen. I can't move. My body is screaming at me to get away from him. Get out. He doesn't love me. Some part of my brain is in agreement but obviously holds little power because I can't speak. I can hardly breathe. All I can do is look at him with wide eyes and a partially open mouth. I feel the muscles of his shoulders are tense underneath my hands. I know he's worried I'm going to flee.

"Tell me, Skyla." His dark, jade eyes are on fire. "Tell me what you want me to do." His eyes never leave mine. I can see the lust he has for me, but what's so shocking is that it's not all I see. There are so many indescribable feelings swimming in them, but there's one that shines through the most.

I don't dare believe it.

There's no way he can love me.

"I... w-want..." I trail off as his eyes bring more emotions forward.

Hope.

He gives me a faint smile.

It all shakes me to my very core. The foundation I'm standing on is weak at best. He's about to destroy me.

I just nod slowly.

"Words, Skyla...," he rumbles dominantly, but not the scary kind. Not the kind that would have me trembling in fear. Not like Thurston.

I grip his shoulders a little more to steady myself. "Don't stop...," I whisper.

His faint smile turns into a wolfish grin. His eyes drop from mine and land directly on the part of me that he's obviously craving. The part of me that's dripping for him, even though I'm terrified of what's about to happen. It's not that I've never had a guy's tongue between my thighs before. It's that the man on the other side of that tongue hasn't bothered to hide his desire for me. Just his grin sends electricity through me, and I know he's about to tear my small little world to the ground brick by brick.

Never letting go of my hips, Dane leans forward and runs his nose along my smoothly waxed pussy. His tongue slowly follows, and I jerk as I gasp when a shock that starts in my clit bursts into a firework that consumes my body.

"Fuck, you taste better than I dreamed," Dane groans. His deep voice sends vibrations through my very soul.

My legs feel like they're going to give out. "Dane…"

Reading me as well as he always does, Dane guides me to his bed. He shifts himself until he's between my legs and helps me sit. "Lean back," he says as he kisses my inner thigh. "Relax." He grabs both of my legs and places them over his shoulders, giving me no choice but to lean back. "Close your eyes." His fingers trail a fiery path from my knees to my hips. I shudder under his touch. "Enjoy this."

I let my eyes fall closed and gasp out a long moan when his tongue finally darts out and circles around my clit. My thighs tighten around him, and my nails dig into the bedspread beneath me. I arch into him.

His tongue slides deep inside me like it was meant to be there. I'd thrust over his tongue, but he's gripping me hard enough to keep me still so I couldn't move if I wanted to. I'm surprised I was even able to arch into him, but it's obvious it's only because he let me.

Hesitantly, I slip my fingers into his hair and bite my lip as I watch him. He said to close my eyes, and I did for a moment, but I like watching him. I don't know how much he'll let me do before he gets upset with me and tells me to just lay here. Like…

I shake my head and squeeze my eyes shut once more. He's not Thurston. He proves it every single day he's around me.

So, I do what he says. I feel. Enjoy. I take a chance and tug him closer to me. Instead of pulling away like part of me expects him to, he moans low again and dives deeper. His tongue is everywhere all at once. Inside me… licking my clit… nipping… biting. My head is spinning.

Before I know what's happening, my body is taking control. With his face buried against my pussy, and his tongue thrusting in and out of me as he vigorously shakes his head, tingles that are not at all familiar to me erupt from my clit. They spread through my pussy as my stomach clenches tight.

"Ah!" I scream because I can't stop it. I try to call his name, but my brain still won't formulate proper words and sentences.

"Holy fuck," he rumbles. "I need you to come for me, Sky. I have to taste all of you."

"Dane!" His name bursts from my lips. Stars explode in front of my eyes, and I'm catapulted into another dimension. My orgasm, one of the few I've ever had and the only one anyone other than myself has given me, rocks through my core and shoots through me.

I arch into him as I spasm. My pussy clenches around his tongue as it pulses erratically. I cry out again and again with each jerk of my hips and shudder that runs through my body until I'm left panting as I fall limp against the bed.

"Oh fuck, Skyla!"

I vaguely hear him shout over the freight train that is my heartbeat. "Oh…" I tremble when I feel something wet hit my stomach.

"I got you," Dane whispers in my ear as his arms wrap around me. He rocks me back and forth with him as he holds me. "You're okay, baby. I got you."

Slowly, the pounding of my heart slows. The jets rumbling through my head fade into the distance. My near hyperventilation gives way to steady breathing. I gradually come down from whatever height he rocketed me to.

"Oh my God," I whisper, gripping his arm like it's a life raft and the only thing stopping me from drowning. The stars that were exploding in front of me eventually give way to my actual surroundings.

Dane's bedroom.

I look down at my stomach, suddenly remembering the wetness, and see Dane's come. I gasp and look at him in wonder. When Thurston came on me like this, it was a punishment. Dane knows that. I told him about it.

So, why does it feel so different when it's Dane's come all over me? Why does it feel more like… a claim?

The thought of what that could mean sends my heart fluttering once more, but I don't have time to think about it before Dane's lips meet mine in a kiss that's so gentle, so loving and passionate, that it makes me want to cry. I melt into him as his hand rubs lightly up and down my arm.

He pulls away slowly and kisses my forehead. Kryptonite. "I'll be right back." He kisses my forehead again, and I melt. Moments later, he's back and cleaning me up with as much love and passion as he threw into every second of the kiss only moments ago.

When he finishes, he helps me get comfortable in his King-sized bed. I melt into the satin sheets as he crawls in next to me. I don't know what happened to the shirt he was wearing or his jeans, but I can't say I care. His skin against mine is comforting and warm. His arms wrapped around me make me feel safe. Like nothing can get through him to me.

"Goodnight, beautiful." His deep voice reverberates through my being. Instead of instilling fear like Thurston's voice did to me, I find solace in it.

I blush furiously at being called beautiful. "Goodnight," I whisper shyly against his arm. I want to call him handsome. I want to call him mine.

I don't do either of those things. Instead, I close my eyes and fall into the deepest sleep I have in more years than I can even remember.

Before my eyes flutter open, the first thing I notice when I wake up is that I've never felt so comfortable in my life. And it's not because of the navy blue satin sheets beneath me. It's because of the sexy cop next to me who's laying on his back with his arm wrapped tightly around me.

I slowly open my eyes. Dane has blackout shades on his window, but a small amount of sun peeks through and lights the room just enough for me to see Dane. The blankets are pushed down to his stomach revealing the tattoo he has on his chest.

'Mi Vida Loca', my crazy life, is Dane's favorite expression. It's a testament to how insane his life has been over the past few years. From thinking his mother was dead, killed in a car crash, to learning she was alive was just the cherry on top of a very messy sundae. He also found out he has two half brothers and some cousins. Alex and Josh share the same mother as he does, and Ryan, Jason, and Nick Crane are all his cousins through Rebekkah, Dane's mother.

It was just after he found all of that out that he got the tattoo across his chest. His arms are covered in them. He's not religious, but he loves crosses. He has a few of them woven into the sleeve tattoos on his arms, and they each have a different meaning to him. I've never asked for details, but I've always wanted to.

I resist the temptation to trace each of his muscles, ridges, and the ink over his body. I know if I do, I'll wake him up. That's the last thing I want. He looks so peaceful, and I'm reeling from what happened last night.

I've never been so calm and relaxed that I fell into a sleep that deep. Not once have I woken up feeling so content. But even with as at peace as I feel right now, I can't stop the doubt that filters in and begins to consume me.

Before I can stop myself, flight instinct kicks in. My chest tightens, and I push myself up. It takes me a second, and Dane's hand dropping to my hip, to realize I'm still completely naked. The idea of that freaks me out. I've slept with a couple of other people in the past few years, not as many as I'm sure Dane and everyone thinks I have, but not once have I woken up naked next to any of them. I've always gone home.

Waking up like this, bare, next to the one man I could fall in love with if I let myself, is too much. Too intimate.

I start to get up as quickly but as gently as I can. I know him well enough to know he won't let me up if he knows I'm trying to flee.

Surprisingly, he barely stirs. When I'm free from his arms, I want to both sob and sigh in relief. I don't do either because I'm too busy holding my breath while I find the clothing he peeled off me last night. I take a last glance at his beautiful face before I snatch my clothes from the floor.

I hurry towards the door and quietly slide my shorts on. Not that I'm worried someone else is here, but I'm not comfortable running around his house naked. Especially since what happened between us can never happen again. I'm way too damaged for a man like him to love me.

"Please tell me we're not still doing this after last night." Dane's raspy voice makes me squeak a little in surprise and spin towards him, eyes wide with my shirt half on. He's sitting up slowly and swinging his legs over the edge of the bed, but his eyes are fixated on me.

"Dane... w-what -"

"What are you doing?" he interrupts before I can finish.

I take a few deep breaths to steady the drumming of my heart as I force myself to finish pulling my shirt down. "I w-was going to..." I look down at my bare feet. "Um... I didn't want to wake you."

Dane makes no effort to stand or walk towards me. Something very opposite of what Thurston would do. I'd be against the wall being choked out by now if I were talking to him.

Instead, Dane clasps his hands together between his legs and leans forward so his elbows are resting on his knees. "Why didn't you want to wake me?"

I raise my head only slightly and bite my lip hard. "I... because...," I stammer over my words as tears sting my eyes. He's too smart to believe my half-lie about not wanting to wake him.

I watch as he slowly stands and walks towards me. His steps are sure and confident, but he doesn't walk any faster. It's like he's trying not to spook a rabbit that he knows is ready to hop away as quickly as she possibly can.

When he stops in front of me, he reaches up and runs his fingers through my hair, then cups my cheek. I lean into his hand as I back towards the door. Like it's a dance, he follows.

"Skyla." His voice makes my mouth dry, and my pussy drip. My stomach clenches, but it's out of desire and need. "Don't. Don't do this. Last night was a huge leap for us. I know you're scared of falling in love again, but you know it's different with me." His tone is like honey. Sweet and kind.

The tears begin to spill. They trail their journey down my cheek. Dane reaches up and wipes them away with the pad of his thumb. He leans in until his lips are just a breath away from mine. My nails dig into the wall my back is against as I close my eyes. I begin to relax slightly and give into my body's need to feel his against mine when someone knocks loudly.

My eyes fly open, and my head snaps towards his bedroom. Suddenly, flashbacks of Thurston's guards pounding on his front door right before they kick it in floods into my mind.

"Skyla!"

Austin.

That's Austin's voice.

My eyes widen. "He can't see us together!" I hiss. I know it's Austin, but my brain works in funny ways. I've never understood how I can know something is one way, but think it's something else. I know that's Austin, but in my head, it's not. It's the guards, and I'm going to get caught doing something wrong.

Cheating.

You're gonna pay for this, bitch! I hear one of the guards yell through the door. *If you think he's not going to know you've tried to get away from him again, you have another thing coming!*

I try to shake the thoughts away. They aren't real. He's not real. Dane. I'm with Dane. Dane is in front of me.

I know what you did, little slut. I squeeze my eyes shut. Thurston's voice thunders through my mind. *I saw the way he looked at you.*

I'm not with Thurston. The logical part of me is fighting hard to help me see the truth in those words, but the part that's overwhelming all of me right now is right back in New York in Thurston's penthouse.

Dane's brows furrow, and his eyes darken. "Why?"

I have no answer. The overpowering sense to flee once more has taken over all of me. I reach for the door handle and fling it open as I shake my head.

I bet you he doesn't kiss like me. Fuck like me. Is that who you want? Some poor asshole who doesn't know how to take care of his little whore?

"Last night -" I look up at him. Dane. It's Dane.

"Was fucking perfect." He takes my hand as I start to dart through the open door.

You know you're paying for all of this once I get my hands on you. Fucking little bitch. You know you're never getting away with this.

I shake my head vigorously as I pull my hand away. "Was a mistake. I can't be with you. It was a mistake. I'm hurting Thurston."

Dane shakes his head. I can see the confusion in them right before I turn away and flee. That little logical voice is screaming at me that I'm not with Thurston. That it's Austin at the door.

But she's locked up tight in her little cell banging on the bars. PTSD has control now.

And she knows she needs to appeal to the guards before Thurston catches her…

Chapter Seven

☙ Dane ☙

"Skyla!" I reach for her hand again, but she slams my own fucking bedroom door behind her.

I close my eyes and let out a breath as I place both hands against the wall. My muscles are flexed. I rest my head against the backs of my hands. I'm ready to run after her, but I know I need to compose myself first.

She kept saying shit about Thurston. I don't need to know anything about her to know that something just triggered a PTSD attack. I've been a cop for a long time. I've seen a lot of shit. Even though her words of last night being a mistake cut me once more, I know the words were said because she's scared and fighting back memories of something he did. She needs calm.

Austin. She needs that familiarity. She needs her brother.

I push off the wall and quickly grab a pair of jeans. I throw on a dark-colored shirt and head downstairs, being purposefully slow and silent. I can hear her sobbing as soon as I open the door to my bedroom. When I reach the bottom of the stairs, I see her sitting on the floor next to the open front door. Austin is wrapped protectively around her and rocking back and forth with her.

I suck in a sharp breath and swallow it because I hate seeing her upset. With everything in me, I want to run to her. It should be me with her in my arms. I should be the one comforting her. I want to be the one she needs for that secure feeling and comfort.

Instead of giving into the need to go to her, though, I give her the time she needs with Austin and walk to the kitchen instead. I grab a glass and fill it with ice before putting filtered water from the door on my fridge into it. After waiting a few minutes, I take the glass with me to her.

Austin still has her wrapped in his arms on the floor. The door is still open. I see Josh walking up my driveway with a bewildered expression darkening his features even more than they are. I take a deep breath and slowly kneel down next to Skyla, but still far enough away not to scare her. Austin is whispering something in her ear that I can't hear.

I clear my throat quietly. "Sky."

Her grip on Austin tightens, and she turns her head into him. "I'm sorry…," she whispers just barely loud enough for me to hear.

I swallow a lump forming in my throat because she sounds so fucking broken. "You don't need to be, baby." I keep my voice steady and low because that's what she needs. Relaxed. Strong. "I have some water for you." I stay right where I am. All of my strength is focused solely on keeping the water in my hand from shaking and betraying my own nerves. I need to be the calm one. I'm always the one who keeps cool under pressure.

"Thank you," she whispers as she reaches for it. She nearly drops it the second I let go, but Austin is quick. He catches it and helps her. I stay right where I am.

I'm no expert in PTSD or the attacks that come with it, but I know enough to know that everyone is different. Some people need to be held and told over and over again that they're safe. It looks like that's what Skyla needs.

Others don't want anyone anywhere near them. And still others just don't want certain people near them. Or objects. Or sounds. I've never seen Skyla in an actual attack. She's told me about a few, but I've never been a part of it. At least not like this. I don't know exactly what she needs from me. I don't know my role, and that's not something my controlling nature likes at all.

"Skyla." I take a deep breath. "Honey, I'm not going anywhere." I may have left her last night after she pushed me away, but I realized something very important.

She's worth it.

She's worth the fight.

No matter what it does to me, she deserves everything. My all.

"I know what I said last night, but I can't walk away from you. You mean way too much to me. You know how I feel about you. I know how you feel about me. If you want to keep pushing me away, I'm going to stand here and show you just how many times I'll walk right back to you. I've done it countless times. I'm not going to stop." I pause and wait for her to look at me. She doesn't, so I continue anyway. "I know what happened. I know it was PTSD. I've gathered it was Austin knocking and calling your name that triggered it."

She sniffles and nods but still doesn't look at me. "I'm so sorry."

"Don't. Don't be. You have no reason to be. Baby, if I can't handle you at your worst, I don't deserve you at your best. So, I guess since I want you, best or worst, I better start proving how caught I am by you, and that I'm not going anywhere. You deserve to be shown how it all can be without the shit you've been through. Support from a huge group of people who are as close to family as anyone could wish for. And someone who loves you the way you should be loved. As just your friend or more. If you just want to be friends, that's gonna suck for me, but I respect you and love you enough to let that be all it is if that's what you want. Because you deserve that. You deserve the entire world and stars."

After a few moments, she looks at me. She smiles softly, then looks up at Josh. He hasn't said a word, but he's not moved from the door. He's been standing there and leaning against the frame like some kind of dark angel.

"I have some news," Josh rumbles, answering the question written all over Skyla's face. "I wish I could say it can wait, but I don't think it can."

I watch Skyla's face fall even further, and it breaks me more than I already am. I look up at Josh. "Not even a couple hours? Let her come down a little?"

Josh shakes his head. "I'd like nothing better than to tell you yes, bro, but I can't. This has the potential to get even more fucked up quick." He looks over his shoulder as his stance shifts to protective mafia boss. I stand, taking my cue from him. Reading us all, Austin pulls Skyla up with him and pulls her further into the safety of the house.

We both relax when we see Lance walking up my sidewalk. "Just me, man. I got that info you wanted printed out."

Josh nods as he turns towards Lance and holds out his hand. "Thanks. See what else you can dig up for me."

"You got it." Lance hands Josh a stack of papers and heads back the way he came.

"What's going on?" I ask, my eyes glued to the papers in his hand as he turns back around.

He shuts the door behind him with a heavy sigh. "You're gonna want to sit down for this. Trust me."

I eye him before nodding and heading for my living room. I sit on an oversized, black, leather chair near the couch where Austin has Skyla settled. Josh sits on the couch that is across from Skyla and on the other side of me.

Skyla wipes her eyes. Austin keeps his arm around her shoulders as we all settle. It's Skyla who breaks the silence. "What's going on?" She asks quietly. "Austin started to say something about you before I flung myself in his arms and we sank to the floor."

I raise an eyebrow as I lean back. "Austin said what?" I ask, curiosity getting the best of me. I know Josh will tell us, but I prefer getting all of the information I can before a bomb is dropped. Less jarring that way.

Josh hands me the stack of papers. "Skyla, what do you know about the Ruthless Warriors?"

I nearly choke as my eyes dart to his. I snatch the papers and start flipping through them as quickly as I can while still comprehending what I'm looking at. "There's no fucking way you're saying what I think you are."

"How I wish there really was no way. But there is," Josh says. "Skyla?"

"I don't..." She looks at me. I can see how confused she is out of the corner of my eye, but I'm too busy flipping through the papers in front of me and mumbling about how fucked up this is. Skyla clears her throat and looks back at Josh hesitantly. "I know what Dane said... They were a biker gang. They tried to hurt Rosie. And I know that the person who went after Raleigh and Harleigh were both members. That's... what... Dane said." She looks at me again.

I drop the papers on the table and lean back once more. I rub my eyes. "This can't be happening."

"What's happening?" Skyla asks, her voice shaking.

Austin lets out a breath and squeezes her shoulder. "First, your head of security was working for Thurston. Um... he's not anymore... Josh took care of him. Second, Josh... thinks... Thurston is part of this Ruthless Warriors gang."

Her beautiful eyes widen, and her head snaps to me. "What?"

I can't help but feel pretty good that she's looking to me to explain this right now. I lean forward and hold my hand out, palm up, inviting her to take it. She looks at it for a few moments before she takes it. I gently pull her to me. She lets out a nervous breath when I pull her in my lap.

"Just give me this, baby. Please. We can talk about it all later, but I need you right here right now. I need to feel you close." I don't add that I also need her to ground me and keep me from tearing out of here and chopping off that fucker's head.

Thankfully, Skyla settles as Josh reaches for the papers. "We thought we eliminated Ruthless Warriors, but Lance got a bit of a hair up his ass after we got home. He started digging into records we have of them. Turns out, Thurston Maxwell just finished his initiation. There was an attack last night on a small business I just acquired." He looks up and directly at Skyla. "At the exact same time the power went out at Lucinio Tech."

He hands her a photograph taken at the scene of an out of control fire near an apartment complex. The business is one I know well. It's a family-owned pizza place that's been in Chicago for decades. I've been getting pizza exclusively there since I ate my first slice of pizza. The business was going under. They took a huge hit when the economy took a downturn. They haven't been able to recover.

"Oh no... That's..." Skyla trails off.

"Luca's." I finish.

"Please tell me no one was in there." Skyla wipes her eyes. I knew she'd ask the question. I hug her tighter because I know the answer.

"Unfortunately, Antonio Luca was there early preparing the dough for the day. He didn't have a chance to get out. There's still an ongoing investigation, but what I got is that they believe it was detonated by remote."

Skyla digs her fingers into my thigh and chokes out a sob. "He pushed something!" she manages to get out before she bursts into tears. She turns to me and grips the waistband of my jeans as she buries her face in my neck. My shirt is about to be soaked, but I don't care about anything but her.

I look at Josh as I wrap around Skyla protectively. He looks just as confused as me, and Austin's mouth is partially open. I don't know if it's because of the fact that I'm hugging his sister like this, or if he's just as bewildered by those words as us.

"What do you mean pushed something?" I whisper in her ear.

Her grip tightens as she sobs. "H-he... w-was... l-looking... a.at... m-me... a-and... p-p-p-pushed... a... ph-phone... b-b-button!"

"Fuck...," I whisper in her silky hair. "I'll -" I'm cut off by Josh's phone.

He answers it as we all watch him. "Yeah." He pauses and glances at me. "Yeah. Hang on." He hands me the phone. "Cole."

I briefly question why he's not calling me, then realize I never grabbed my phone when I threw these jeans on. I just came down here with the intention of proving to Skyla that I'm not like Thurston, and that I'm not going anywhere, despite how hurt I am or become. She's worth it. She's worth all the pain, happiness, and far more.

I take the phone. "I thought you'd be sleeping."

"Planned on it, but I had a hunch. Came into the office. Hunch didn't play out, but fuck if I didn't stumble on something. Need to know what you make of it, though."

"Josh is here. He just dropped a motherfucking bomb. What could possibly be worse than finding out the Ruthless Warriors still breathe?"

"No shit? Well, this makes a lot more fucking sense now. Did Josh tell you about the fire at Luca's?"

"Yeah. Just now. Along with a lot of other shit."

"I found something at the scene. Arson investigators are still combing through it, but I have the remains of what I think is a bomb. I called out the Bomb Squad to make sure it wasn't going to blow up in my face."

"We think Thurston detonated it from the chopper. Skyla just said she saw him push something on what looked like a phone." I rub her back as she hiccups. She's still burrowed as close to me as she can be, but at least the sobs have stopped.

"Well, I'm pretty sure that's what it was, but there's more."

"I don't think I can handle more."

"You can handle this. Trust me. The bomb did its job, but it didn't totally take out the casing. You can still make out some etching. Guess what it says."

I close my eyes. "Ruthless Warriors."

"You got it. And guess where it was made."

I raise an eyebrow unsure where he's going with this. "China."

Cole laughs. "Man, you'd think. But no. I got a buddy in the lab to help me out with this. He pushed aside something else he's working on because he was just as curious as me. The casing was definitely melted. I was able to see the Ruthless Warriors shit pretty clearly, but this other thing had my dick hard. I knew I was onto something huge. It was made in London."

I stiffen and hold Skyla tight enough to make her squeak and look at me with wonder in her eyes. "Mother...fucker..."

"Yep. T-Rac Merc."

"You're fucking kidding. You have to be." My throat has gone completely dry, and I cough.

"Nope. Not even a little bit."

"Christ." I can't breathe. "Jesus Christ. Josh just told us that Lance found out Thurston Maxwell just completed his initiation for the Ruthless Warriors. We thought we took them out. We fucking didn't. Tits wasn't the leader. He couldn't have been because they've multiplied like fucking spiders."

"And his initiation was blowing up Luca's," Cole finishes, like a mind reader. "Why?"

"No fucking clue. When I catch him, I'll ask him right before I rip his fucking throat out and feed it to him," I growl dangerously.

"Save that aggression for finding him, Lieutenant."

I thrust Josh's phone back at him. I know my eyes have darkened because Skyla is stroking my chest soothingly, but also hiding her face. She hates anger. It's a trigger, and I've always done well at hiding it from her.

I run my fingers through her hair as I take a deep breath. Using her to calm me, I turn my head and kiss her neck. I tune out everything else going on around me until I feel Austin touch my knee to get my attention.

"He's not done ruining our lives yet," Austin says with a wry smile and dry chuckle as he nods at Josh. He knows Josh wouldn't do something like that. He's all about fixing things, but I don't blame him for feeling like his life is being turned upside down. It literally is.

"I've come up with a plan," Josh starts. I already don't like it. Just by reading the expression on his face, I can tell he's hesitant to even bring it up. Josh doesn't hesitate. Ever.

"Just spit it out. How bad can it be? Can't be worse than everything we just found out." I trust Cole told him everything he told me as soon as I gave him his phone back.

Josh takes a breath and looks at his hands. His elbows are resting on his knees, and his hands are clasped between them. "We need to flush him out. He's obsessed with Skyla. Best way to make him come out of the hiding place he's crawled into is make him think he'll never get her back."

"He's never getting her back as it is." Austin says.

I furrow my brows. "Where are you going with this?"

Josh doesn't look up. "I hear Vegas is nice this time of year."

Skyla's head whips around so fast, I'm convinced she gave herself whiplash, but I'm with her. "You can't possibly mean what I think you do," I say through gritted teeth.

Josh finally looks up. Austin's jaw is, once again, clenched tight. Josh shrugs. "You know as well as I do a claim is going to push him off that ledge."

"I still don't agree with this!" Austin nearly screams as he stands. "Are you fucking crazy? Why not just buy a fucking ring and put it on her finger? You guys are rich enough. Pay off a judge. Fake the license! Why do it for real?"

"I thought about all of that, Austin," Josh says calmly as he looks up at Skyla's protective brother. "The truth is, I could do that. The problem, though, is no matter how good Lance can fake shit, there's always a small chance that someone will figure it out. I don't leave anything to chance, and I don't fucking believe in luck. The marriage can be annulled, but this needs to happen. As long as he thinks Skyla is his, he'll stay in hiding until he's ready to come out and play. We don't want that. We want him to play with us on our terms. We want him to come out when we want him to. Not when he's good and ready."

"I'm a possession to him," Skyla whispers. She shifts just enough to let me know that she wants to sit up. While I don't let her go, I do loosen my grip enough so she can do just that. She looks up at Austin. "He's right, Austin. Thurston doesn't like when his toys are taken away. He likes the control. If we can force him out, he loses control, and it makes his decision making, well, unhinged, I guess. Unpredictable for him, but predictable for us. He'll come after me."

"But we'll be ready," Josh finishes. His words ease my racing mind because I know my brother and trust him with my life.

I can't say Austin feels the same way.

"This... I..." Austin scrubs his hands down his face before looking back at Josh as he collapses back on the couch. "How? How do we pull off a fake marriage that's fucking real?"

"Simple," I say with a shrug. "We go to Vegas. We get it done."

"But you two will literally be married." Austin shakes his head. "She's not ready for that. You know that. You saw what happened this morning."

Once more, I give him a shrug. "Like Josh said, marriages can be annulled if that's what Skyla wants." I don't say me, because the more I think about it, the more I want this. I want to call Skyla my wife.

"We'll have to have rules," Skyla says as she looks over her shoulder at me.

I just hug her tighter. "Any rules you want."

"Rule number one. No falling in love. We treat this like a business deal."

I raise an eyebrow and ignore the fact that it feels like she kicked me in the chest. I say nothing at all as she turns away from me. She stands and heads to my office mumbling something about a notepad.

When she's out of sight, I let out the breath I was holding. "Too late for that," I say only loud enough for Austin and Josh to hear.

I hear Austin gasp a little bit. Josh grins, but none of it matters.

All that matters right now is figuring out all of the ways I'll be breaking her rules.

Chapter Eight

☙ Skyla ☙

Dane hands me a glass of white wine as he sits down on the patio chair across from me. I take the glass and look down at it. I'm pretty sure it's too early to drink, it's not even noon, but Dane knows me very well, apparently. I don't need to think about time. I just need to relax and pretend life doesn't exist.

I need him.

Him.

In whatever way I get him.

"So, the morning was definitely fucked up," Dane says, breaking into my intrusive thoughts. He takes a drink of the chilled wine.

I shrug and continue to stare into the contents of the glass. "Yeah."

After a few moments, Dane sets his glass on the table and leans forward. The breeze picks up a little, and I'm struck for the billionth time how much better everything is in the Crane and Lucinio compound. It's peaceful. Almost a totally different universe from the city. Even the air seems cleaner.

Dane wraps both of my hands in his, even though I'm still holding the glass. "Please talk to me."

I let out a long breath and study our hands. "It's just… so much, you know? I'm… still… trying to wrap my head around last night." I swallow the sudden lump in my throat. "I just… I… don't… know what to do." I sniffle and try to pull my hands free, but Dane just holds them tighter. I glance up at him before dropping my eyes again.

"Skyla, honey, I know how scary all of this is for you. But I've never hidden how I feel about you. Even with how many times you've pushed me away. I fucked up last night when I walked away. It was me showing my own vulnerabilities. It hurts every time you shut down on me, Sky, but my biggest fuck up was thinking for a second that the best decision was to walk away. I'll take the heartbreak every day if it means you're in my life."

I chuckle a little, but I won't deny that the words make my heart skip a beat. "That almost sounds like a proposal."

He smiles and lets go of my hands only long enough to put my wine cup on the table next to me. He brings my hands to his lips and kisses them. "Shall I get down on one knee?" He gives me a teasing grin that I'd never let him know makes my insides melt.

"How about just a promise that no matter how crazy I get, you'll be there to bring me down and convince me that you'll still be here."

"Done. That can be rule number one of this fake marriage contract because I sure as fuck ain't agreeing to the one you came up with." He kisses my hands again before letting them go. He takes the notepad I found in his office and the pen I have clipped to it. He turns it towards him and crosses off rule number one. "I'm already in love with you. Have been for a long time. And so have you. So, this one is a moot point."

"I was… probably… still in panic mode."

Dane nods. "Don't doubt that." He starts writing. "Prove each day how much I love you."

I blush. "You're going to strike down all of them, aren't you?"

He just grins. "Rule number two. Public displays of affection stay in public. Not at home." He taps the pen against his chin. "I'll agree to that for the most part. With one addendum." He crosses out part of the rule and starts writing something else. I squeeze my legs together because his contract talk turns me on as much as he does. "Not at home is struck. But I will agree to taking things at your pace. I'm not going to agree to not touching you or holding your hand or kissing you. But I will take things slow."

"But what if things start going too fast and -"

Dane shakes his head. "Stop. You and I have cuddled while watching movies. We've been in some pretty intimate positions as friends. And you've been comfortable in them until you start overthinking everything. I'm not asking for changes in that aspect of things. It all remains the same. The only difference between now and then is we've crossed a line that involved my tongue in your pussy. So, I reserve the right to not let you run this time." He looks back down. "Sleeping in separate rooms."

"Not negotiable," I say quickly. I know if we're in the same room, things will happen that I'm not certain I'm ready for. And I won't be able to stop it because he has a way of making me want to tear off my clothes and stand in front of him bare begging him to do with me as he pleases. That's dangerous.

He's dangerous.

He crosses it off and starts writing something else. I try to grab his hand as I lean in to see what he's doing, but with one dominant look, he both silences the words on my tongue and has me sitting down like a good girl just staring at him with doe eyes.

"Same bedroom."

I shake my head vigorously. "You said my pace." I clutch my chest. I'm going to have a heart attack. My heart is speeding faster than a Nascar racer.

"I did. But we've slept in the same bed, Skyla. Numerous times, last night not included. And I've always made sure to respect your wishes and boundaries. That's not changing."

"Then I sleep in the big chair you have by the window."

He shakes his head. His eyes never leave mine. "No deal."

"Then pillows between us! Final offer."

"Nope. We've never needed them. A ring and vows doesn't change that. I'm never going to force you to do anything. Last night should prove that. Nothing I did last night was against your will. And you know if you'd told me to stop, I would have. I'm not changing anything we're used to for the sake of you closing your heart to me again. I'm not letting it happen. I got through a wall last night. I'm not going to go backwards."

I take my wine glass and down it all in one gulp. My hands are shaky and clammy. "Dane, we have to -"

"To let things progress naturally. Stop throwing up blockades in between us. Agree? Or not?" He casually refills my glass.

I take a more civilized sip before putting the glass down and dropping my head in my hands. "Fine. Agree."

Dane nods. "Next. No flirting with other people. I'll agree to that." He takes a drink of his wine and chuckles. "No telling anyone it's fake. We don't know who to trust." He looks up at me. "I'll agree to that, but I think family is excluded. Your brother knows. Josh swore him to secrecy because we don't know much about his girl. I think the rest of the family is safe, but it stays between the family. No one outside of it, including guards."

"Agree to that."

Dane writes that down, and the fact that he's taking this so seriously makes me want to jump him. "Attend events together as a couple is kind of a given," I say softly about the next one on the list.

"Yep. Agree to that one. We have a family charity event coming up." He grins. "Next is drive you to work every day on my way into headquarters."

I bite my lip and let my hair fall over my cheek to hide my blush. "Non-negotiable."

"Happy to oblige that one. I'd like to add lunch together whenever possible. I know things get busy for us both, but that's something I'd enjoy."

I nod and smile a little. "Agreed."

He writes that down. "Next up. Send flowers once a week."

I look up at him shyly. "I've never had anyone send flowers before. Not even Thurston."

He raises an eyebrow. "No one has ever given you flowers?"

I shake my head. "I had a secret admirer once in high school. I don't know if your school did it, but ours had a couple times a year where you could send a chocolate rose to someone. I never found out who sent it, and it never happened again."

"That's... I can't even fathom that. Not sending a woman you love flowers is a damn crime."

He says it with such conviction that I giggle and blush even more. "You can take that one off. It's stupid. It makes it an obligation."

"It doesn't make it an obligation, and it's staying." He looks down again. "Bring dinner to each other if one of us has to work late in the office." He nods again as he looks up at me. "Agreed. Sometimes, I know you do dinner meetings with Alex, and I'm out dealing with warrants and shit, but this is good if we're in office."

"It's also… well, I mean, it's kind of a way to keep me from being alone. Alone is when I think too much."

"It's also when things happen. Even if you're here, you're still going to have people around. So, I definitely agree to this, but not just to keep you from being alone. This allows me to spend more time with you."

I take another sip of my wine before setting it down carefully. "You probably won't like the next one too much." I look down waiting for him to veto it.

He chuckles a little. "Why would I have a problem with this one?"

I shrug a little weakly. "Because it… takes… away from your time with your family. I know that's valuable to you." I shake my head and reach for the notepad. "That one was silly."

He quickly removes it from my reach leaving me gawking at him. "I fail to understand how a movie night with the girl of my dreams one night out of the week where she gets to pick the movie and food is a bad thing. I spend plenty of time with my family. My question is why is this something that's contract worthy? It seems like this is a given."

I quickly look down and sigh. It takes me a full minute to answer, but Dane is so incredibly patient. "It's… because I never got to do that with Thurston. I've gotten really used to it with you when we have movie nights. I don't want it to change."

"Baby girl, that's not changing. But I'll keep it in here just to give you peace of mind. Same with this next one. Date night once every two weeks. I'll keep it at that because I know how busy we can both get, but I reserve the right to more if time allows." He starts writing that down.

My lip trembles at the utter sweetness he's showing. "Agreed."

"Next. No sexual advances, touches, or acts." He looks up at me. His jade eyes become dark depths of dominance that have my thighs shifting again and moving together to give me the friction I need but know won't ease the ache. "You really want me to agree to that? That's going to be torture for you, Skyla. Because I'll do very unfair shit. Like shower with the door open and walk around naked."

My eyes widen impossibly. "Dane!"

"I'll jack off in front of you and ask you how badly you want it because there's nothing in here saying teasing is off the table."

"Oh my God, you're impossible." I, as casually as I can, drop my hand between my thighs and cup my pussy praying to anyone listening on either side of the line to please keep me from coming. Thankfully, the table itself isn't glass. It's wood and you can't see through cracks because there aren't any.

Unfortunately for me, Dane is way too observant. His eyes drop to the table. I know right away he knows what's happening. I both hate and love that just one night with his magic tongue has opened the floodgates. I hate it because it means I'm not going to be able to fight it and just quietly go to the bathroom to relieve the tension. Yet, I love it because he's the only one who has ever made me feel like this and react like this.

Maybe that's a bad thing, too. Maybe I just hate it all the way around.

Dane meets my eyes once more as he sits up straighter. "Come here," he says raspily as he crooks his finger at me.

Of its own traitorous accord, my body obeys. I clasp my hands together in front of me and wait for his next command like a puppy who hangs off my master's every word. I feel like I should be panting and wagging my tail.

My insides tremble, but as he looks me up and down like a feral, rabid animal, I feel my pussy get wetter.

After he gets his fill, he meets my hooded eyes once more. "You have two choices. Sit down on my lap and let me solve the problem you find yourself experiencing right now. Or tell me you want me to agree to the nothing sexual bullshit that is only on here because you're fucking afraid you're gonna become even more addicted to me like I am you."

His voice takes on the dominant edge that I love so much, but it's the lining of pure possessive asshole that has me pulling down my pants and sitting on his lap. It takes an immense level of strength I wasn't aware I possessed to keep my shirt on.

His hand travels up my thigh like it's meant to be there; like it's his. He has no idea just how much I want it to be. How much I want him to take complete control and tell me I'm his. Maybe this wedding won't be such a bad idea after all. Fake or not, I'll have the choice to stay in it, won't I? I didn't put that in the contract. Will he? Maybe I should.

He stops and lets his fingers stroke my already soaked pussy. "So, should we strike this?"

I nod. "Strike it."

"Good girl." He slides two fingers inside me with no warning and thrusts in and out of me hard and slow.

"Oh, Dane!" I cry out.

He presses his lips against my neck and crosses out the rule he saw right through. I hold the paper still for him but only because I need to think about something, anything other than how good his big, thick, and long fingers feel inside me.

"Last. No secrets. I'll agree to that."

"Dane…" My eyes flutter closed, and I thrust against his fingers as my thighs tremble. My pussy pulses erratically and makes sounds that I'm certain would make me blush if I wasn't trying to keep myself from coming so fast. I moan and let my head drop against his shoulder.

"Anything else?" He twists his fingers slowly and crooks them.

Fuck yes. Finger fucks every day. Sex in every room of the house on every surface. Back massages that end with your tongue in my pussy. Let me do the housewife stuff for you. All I ask for in return is you love me forever and let me ride you like a bull whenever I want.

"That… we… can… stay… married… if we want…," I pant. He hits the right spot inside me and starts rubbing my clit with his thumb. "Dane!" My hips thrust into his fingers on their own, matching his rhythm.

"I'll agree to that."

I feel his other arm moving against me as he writes, but it's the fingers inside me that have so easily found my spot that have my attention. He plays me like a violin and hurdles me into the unknown. I tighten around his fingers like a vice. He can't move his fingers anymore, but he can still crook them.

"Ah! Dane!"

"Look at me. I want to see you when I let you come."

I do as I'm told as his pressure on my clit increases until he reaches the perfect mixture of rubbing and crooking against my spot. "Ah!

Fuck! Please! Please let me come, Dane! Please!" My hips jerk uncontrollably against him.

"Good girl. Come for me now. Eyes on me."

I grip the wrist of the hand with the fingers buried inside me and throw my head back. If I could howl, I probably would. I'm sure I look like I'm about to. Despite that, though, my eyes never leave his. I let my head fall back just enough so that my eyes are still on him.

"Fuck! Dane! Yes! Yes!" I arch into him so hard that his fingers slide impossibly deeper. I come so hard that I can feel myself soaking his fingers. It drips down my thighs onto his jeans. I cry out his name again and again with each and every spasm my pussy makes; each jerk of my hips.

I want to let my eyes fall closed, but I don't. I love the look he's giving me. The cockiness, possessiveness, and pride swimming in his eyes makes my orgasm that much more powerful. I know I'm in trouble. I'll never be able to walk away from him. He has the power in his hands to either send me to the moon or destroy me forever.

Whatever comes from here on out, I know one thing…

…I'm already his.

Chapter Nine

 Dane

(One Week Later)

"You may kiss your bride!" the Elvis performing our wedding says right before he starts singing *Burning Love* and doing all the hip gyrating that the King did himself.

I brush Skyla's hair out of her face as I lean down. She smiles softly, her blue eyes sparkling like the ocean. I press my lips against hers, softly at first, then a little harder until we're both consumed by the kiss. I hug her tighter. The whistles and cheers quickly fade. I feel like we're spinning through the air of our own little planet.

When I finally pull away, the applause comes back like a freight train. My heart skips more than a few beats as what we just did sinks in. This might be just for appearances, but we're legally married right now for the foreseeable future. At the very least, until this is over.

The most? The rest of our lives.

We're still navigating the new relationship dynamic, so being married right now seems surreal.

Backwards.

I tangle my fingers in Skyla's hair and keep my arm locked around her waist as I sway gently. "You okay?"

"Too late not to be."

I kiss her forehead and keep my lips pressed against her head. "It's gonna be okay. Nothing changes. We're still taking things at your pace. I'm still proving to you that you're safe with me. That I'm not going to hurt you. Right?"

She nods and lets out a breath. Her arms circle my waist, and I feel her relax more and more. "Maybe I just need to get out there and show those machine's who's boss."

I grin and hug her a little tighter. "I'm very much down for that." I pull away and plaster a smile on my face. I can feel her nervousness. It's my job to ease it.

I let my hand snake down her arm until it reaches hers and entwines with it. I squeeze it and lead her up the aisle. She puts her other hand over mind and sticks close to me. The Elvis impersonator keeps singing and performing, sending us away with good vibes that make us both laugh.

Over the past week, we've been both planning our little ceremony while making sure that the announcement we're getting married was plastered all over the place. The media has been in a frenzy just because of the way the story was spun.

Lucinio Tech's Princess Is Getting Hitched!
Chicago Police Department's Bad Boy Off The Market!
Gorgeous CFO of Lucinio Tech Falls For The Bad Boy!
Alex Lucinio's Pretty CFO Stole Lieutenant Michaels' Heart!
And my personal favorite…
Chicago's Princess Tames CPD's Beast!

I don't know who came up with that headline, but they deserve a fucking raise. Since the first headline dropped, Ryan and Josh have been hard at work giving details we want known, and keeping details we don't want known out. They even made sure to link Skyla with Thurston Maxwell by saying she was previously his girlfriend. They gave a nice touch by suggesting a split due to nefarious actions on Mr. Maxwell's part.

And just as we wanted, Thurston himself got involved by giving an interview to some of the largest news networks in the nation and world. He had to do some type of damage control. It's really too bad for him that his money doesn't go as far as ours. Or rather, the fear factor we have compared to what he does. The power and control. Everyone knows not to mess with Ryan Crane or Josh Lucinio. It wouldn't be in anyone's best interest.

"How do you feel?" Josh asks when he and everyone else meet us in the lobby of The Little White Chapel.

"Nervous. And like I need to go lie down," Skyla says. "I mean we were doing really well. Working things out. Taking things slow. I was getting used to the whole thing with lots of security everywhere I go. I never complained. I was comforted. I am. I am comforted. I feel safe and amazing. But… this…" She waves her hand around the lobby. We all smile because we know exactly what she means.

"Well, we're in Vegas. Go let loose. Have fun. Leave everything else to us," Ryan says from behind me. He has his arm around his wife, Arianna, and is holding his son's, Christopher's hand. He knows just how to take minds of drama and put them where they should be.

Skyla smiles softly before launching herself at him. Jason and Nick Crane, Ryan's brothers, stand next to him with their wives. Jason is holding his son, Jackson. Chase Shaw is here with his wife, Breetana. Cole is here. Gavin and his wife, Harleigh, are here. Even Alex and Raleigh have flown in from their honeymoon just for this occasion.

While we wanted to make a huge show of doing it fast, we also needed it to look legit. There's no way either of us would get married without those close to us. Lance and Damon. Austin with his girl, Racheal. I am unsure if we can trust her or not. She's the only one here who has no idea this is all for show.

As Ryan whispers something in Skyla's ear that somehow makes all the tension leave her petite body, I'm suddenly hugging another tiny blonde. Taylor Reddick, my best friend, grins as he shakes my hand while his wife, Nicole, hugs me as hard as she possibly can.

"I know what this is, but I'm still so happy for you," she whispers just loud enough for me to hear.

I kiss the top of her head. "Thank you, sweetheart."

Taylor pulls me in for a hug and pats my back. "She's a keeper," he rumbles as he pulls back.

"Don't I know it." I reach down and pull their six-year-old son, Tait, into a hug before letting him go and hugging Jordan and Harper, my six-year-old adopted brother and sister.

When I stand again, my dad is right there to hug me. "I'm proud of you, son."

I chuckle as I hug him back. "Don't be too proud. Yet anyway. She could still run away."

"She won't," my mom, also Alex's and Josh's mom, says. "I really think she'll stick around."

I hug her as my eyes meet Skyla's. She blushes and smiles. We agreed that we wouldn't wear tuxes and dresses, but I can't help but drool over the simple white skirt and tank top paired with the strappy white sandals she's wearing. She's perfect.

The clicking of cameras and flash photography happening around us snaps me back to reality. I'd almost gotten lost enough in her to forget completely about the media we've allowed in to help us with this fucked up charade. The real reason we're doing this isn't out of love. It's out of necessity to protect her.

My girl.

I clear my throat and hold out a hand for her. "We should clear out. I'm sure there are other people waiting to get married by Elvis." I grin, putting on a show for the cameras.

She takes my hand, and I kiss her ring. It's a simple gold band that matches the one on my finger. We both agreed anything flashy is pointless unless we're really going to give this a go. Even though I want to see this work, it's the one thing I didn't argue with her on. I could see how important that was to her. When she said we'd pick out better rings that fit us more if we chose to stay together, that gave me enough to hold onto.

I lead her out to the waiting white, stretch limo. It's the one thing about this day that I wouldn't compromise on, and I'm glad I didn't. It's sweltering here today, and I have no intention of walking in this heat four miles to the MGM Grand, where we're all staying. I also really want the time by ourselves. Our security detail, including Ryan and Josh, will be following us, but the limo itself, driven by one of Lucinio Mafia's guards, is all for us.

As everyone throws birdseed in the air, we both duck and laugh as we run towards the waiting limo. She practically dives in. I'm grateful I'm behind her because I'm certain she forgot she was wearing a rather short skirt. I'm not unhappy about the view I got of her pretty lace panties, but damn if I'm letting anyone else have the privilege.

Once she's safely inside, I hop in after her and close the door.

"MGM, sir?" the guard asks from the driver's seat. "Or would you like to do the tour of Hoover Dam now?"

"Nah," I say. "We've got a few days. Let's go check in."

"Yes, sir." The guard grins as the partition goes up.

I waste absolutely no time turning and kissing my girl with the level of passion I couldn't in that chapel. I've been good and let her take the lead with this, but she's always put the brakes on before it's gone too far. The last time I had my fingers inside her was the day we hashed out the rules of this relationship. When she said she wanted to take things slow, I didn't realize she'd want to take five steps back.

Still, I've never pushed her, and I won't. I'm happy she still lets me kiss her until her toes curl.

I drop my hand to her thigh and trail my fingertips up and under her skirt. I feel her stiffen slightly. I expect her to grab my wrist to stop me like she usually does, but she doesn't. Instead, she relaxes, and my heart jumps. She parts her legs for me. It's all the invitation I need. I push her already soaked panties aside and tease her clit with my thumb.

"Mmm," she moans into my mouth. She grabs my wrist and pushes my hand closer and arches into me.

I smile against her lips. "I love when you do that." I slide two fingers inside her because I want nothing more than relieve that ache and make her come.

My favorite things in the world are her pussy clenching around my fingers as I pump them inside of her, and the way she looks when she comes. The soft smile she gets on her face, the pretty blush, and the way her eyes roll back as she tries to keep them open make me hard as steel in nanoseconds.

Her hips jerk as she grips my wrist tighter and starts riding my fingers. "When I do what?"

I grin and lean forward as I thrust my fingers inside of her. "When you arch into me." I press my lips against her throat. "When you moan for me." I thrust harder and faster as I give her clit the perfect amount of pressure while I rub it. "And when you let me take the edge off while allowing me to watch you come."

"Oh…," her voice rumbles against my lips as I kiss her throat and to the side of her neck. She tangles the fingers of her other hand into my hair and tugs as she begins to grind herself into my fingers.

I can feel the very second she's about to lose it, and I want nothing more than for her release to be while I'm licking her. I continue to thrust my fingers inside her hard, deep, and fast while twisting them and driving her insane. She's trying so hard to stay quiet, but I know that's not going to last. Skyla is a screamer.

I pull my fingers out of her and replace them with my tongue. As soon as she feels my breath against her, her hand is over her mouth. She tugs my head closer until my face is buried in her sweet pussy. I pinch her clit before rubbing it at the same pace I'm tongue fucking her. Her pussy clamps around my tongue, and I moan low, sending vibrations all through her.

She screams and jerks hard and uncontrollably into me. Taking my moan as her command to release, just like I want her to, she comes hard for me, her pussy pulsing so beautifully. Her thighs tremble as I slow my licks. I rub her clit slower and slower, helping her come down.

When I feel us turning and slowing down, I give her a last lick and adjust her panties. She's panting into her hand with her eyes closed. I take the few seconds we have left to suck her off my fingers.

"Fuck, Dane. How am I supposed to resist you when you do things like that?"

I shrug and wink teasingly. "Stop resisting me. That's a start."

She swats me as she laughs. "Insufferable."

"Irresistible," I correct. I catch her hand and kiss it just as someone opens the door.

Josh pops his head in. "Alright, lovebirds. Ryan and I are going to flank you. Guards will be everywhere. It's going to look a lot like the President of the United States is arriving. We even have snipers."

Skyla's mouth drops slightly. "Isn't that a little overkill?"

"Nope," Josh says. "We don't know how much power he's amassed. All we know is the Ruthless Warriors are still fucking out there resurrecting from the dead. Not taking chances. Besides, the game is showing the level of power we have compared to him. We know he's cocky enough to not care, though, and that's what we want."

"Trust us, honey," Ryan says, appearing at the door. "We've been in the game a long time. No one is going to hurt you. Your job is to have fun while we're here and put on a show for the cameras. Our job is to keep you both safe."

"Did our family get in safe?" I ask.

"Yep. They're being escorted as we speak," Josh says. "Time to go."

I nod and take Skyla's hand in mine. I get out of the limo and help her. Several of our thousands of guards are grabbing luggage. Others are surrounding us. Others are escorting the rest of the family into the hotel. I glance around and spot the snipers right off. They're positioned in several different places. I'm sure we even have a couple on the roof of this hotel. Josh and Ryan don't take any chances. Especially when it comes to their family.

So, with my cousin and brother flanking us, just as they said they would, and other guards surrounding us, I let myself feel like a goddamn King. And the Queen of my heart is the gorgeous woman at my side gripping my hand tightly. The woman I hope I get to keep forever.

A few minutes later, I'm opening the door to our suite. We stay in the hall with Ryan and Josh as guards sweep the room. When they finish, I guide her inside. I'm excited for her to see the room. She's traveled a lot, but the one place she's never been and always wanted to go to is Las Vegas. She specifically begged Josh to let us stay at the MGM because it's been one of her dreams. He made it work.

She spins in a slow circle as she takes in everything. The modern decor, the floor to ceiling window overlooking the strip, and the ensuite kitchen. I follow her with a grin as she walks to the bedroom. There's a jacuzzi tub in there that I asked to have filled. I asked for some relaxing oils to be added and some pink carnation petals to be floating on top of the water. They're her favorite.

When we enter the room, though, both of us are taken aback by the bucket filled with ice and a chilling bottle of wine. I didn't order that. And I certainly didn't order the carnation petals on the bed in the shape of a heart with a suspicious looking box in the middle of it that's wrapped up in silver and pink paper.

Skyla looks up at me and blinks. "What is -"

I shake my head. "Not anything I did. I swear."

She turns back to the box and tilts her head. "It has a card…"

I approach it cautiously and lean in just enough to see what it says. I blink and then start laughing. "Oh my fucking God. It's Lyric's doing."

Skyla laughs and picks up the card. She starts reading out loud. "Congratulations on finally making a hell of a move, D! Finally! And Skyla, let me know if he gets all grumpy bear on you. I'll fly up there and kick his butt!" She pauses as she laughs. "I've always liked her. She's sassy."

"She's a fucking brat. But we all love her." I grin.

Skyla continues reading. "We got you some treats that we hope you both enjoy. Congrats again! Lyric, Matt, DJ, and the kids. P.S. There might be a few naughty surprises in there. Maybe. Don't do anything I wouldn't do!"

"I don't want to know what her devious mind came up with. Especially if Matt and DJ were any help."

Skyla giggles as she starts opening the box. "Oh! They got us chocolates and chocolate covered strawberries. I knew I loved her for a reason. She knows I love chocolate!"

I lean over to look and then kiss her neck as I pull up the top part of the box. It's too deep to just be treats. Sure enough, underneath is tissue paper. Skyla removes it and drops the box back on the bed with wide eyes.

I crack up. "Still love her?" I move to her side and set the chocolates down. "Let's see. We have some furry handcuffs. Pink. Just for you, I'm sure." I grin at her. She blushes a deep shade of red as I turn my attention back to the goodies that have piqued my interest. "Four matching silver silk ties. I'm gonna say that's for me."

Skyla squeaks out a laugh. "What would you even do with those other than wear them?"

I grin even wider. "Well, you see, pretty girl," I tease. "These are much more comfortable on your hands and legs then those cuffs would be."

She squeaks again, but this time it's in shock. "Dane, no!"

"In time, baby." I pull out a blindfold that's silver to match those ties. "And that would be to blindfold you with. Oh shit." My eyes widen, and I bite back a laugh.

Skyla is quicker than me. She grabs a small, pink, bullet looking vibrator and pink dildo that looks suspiciously about the size of my dick.

As Skyla goes about shoving everything in the box and hiding under the blankets on the bed, I take out my phone as a conversation and the image of a mischievous glint in Lyric's eye plays in my mind.

Dane: When you said 'hypothetically speaking, how big is your dick?' And I answered you only after grilling you about why, it was so you could customize this wedding gift to the literal size of my dick for Skyla, wasn't it?

Seconds later, I have my answer.

Lyric: Well, in all fairness, you might like to get pegged. So, it could be for you.

Dane: Holy fuck, you're such a brat. We're not speaking.

I grin as I put my phone back in my pocket. Lyric will know I'm kidding, and when I look at my phone later, I'm sure there will be more than a couple of texts in response to that.

Skyla is staring at me in both wonder and awe and probably a little bit of shock. "What possible reason would she have to do that?"

"Oh, baby girl. You know what a matchmaker Lyric is. She's been trying to set us up since she first met you. Go look in the bathroom. There's a surprise in there that really is from me."

Skyla's pretty blue eyes brighten. She turns and scurries into the bathroom. I follow and lean against the doorframe with my arms folded across my chest. A soft smile plays on my face as I watch her. She spins around, and jumps on me. I'm rewarded with the biggest and sweetest hug I've gotten out of her in a very long time. I do the only thing I can and tighten my grip as I bury my face in her botanical scented hair.

"Thank you. For everything."

I smile and kiss her neck. "Enjoy your bath. Toss your clothes out here. I'll lay out an outfit for you to change into, and we can play a couple machines after dinner. You have two hours."

"Mmm… Sounds heavenly."

I reluctantly let her go and turn around. I head for the suite to grab our luggage that I heard our guards bring in a few minutes ago and leave by the door.

I take my time to give Skyla privacy, but there's nothing I'd like more right now than to be in that water with her.

A few minutes later, I peek into the bedroom and see her clothes neatly folded on the bed. I chuckle as I walk back into the room. Skyla is happily relaxing in the jacuzzi tub. I put her suitcase on the bed and silently rummage through to find the outfit I want her to wear. A pair of skinny black jeggings with a deep red, short sleeve shirt. It dips down to give her just enough cleavage to make my mouth water for her all night long, but it's conservative enough that she won't feel uncomfortable. I pick out a sexy little red silk bra and matching panties to go with it.

After I lay it out for her and put the outfit she was just wearing away, I can't help but smile, despite the danger lurking. Skyla Winters is my wife. How fucking lucky am I?

Chapter Ten

❦ Skyla ❦

As soon as we finish dinner at Craftsteak with the family, we all walk the block back to the MGM. Dane takes my hand and kisses it like it's the most natural thing for him to do. Like he's really not faking any of this for the cameras. Not that I am. I'm just not used to the idea of someone actually being genuinely interested in me.

Not counting Thurston, every guy I've been with has only wanted one thing from me. I'm pretty, so they want sex. When they get it, they're gone. I'm successful, so all they want from me is money. I work for powerful people, so all they want from me is a way to my boss. No matter the relationship, it's always been one of those three things that they've wanted.

I thought it would be different with Thurston. He was more successful than me. My boss. So he wasn't trying to get to himself through me. He didn't need my money. He had plenty of his own. He made me feel like while he thought I was pretty, it didn't matter to him. He didn't pressure me into sleeping with him. Right off the bat, that was something very different with him. Even though people thought I slept with him to get my position, we both knew the truth and didn't care.

Looking back, I know it was all an act. I didn't realize until almost the very end that he not only destroyed me personally, but also professionally. I was known as the girl who fucked the boss to get to the top.

"Hey," Dane rumbles against my fingertips, breaking me from my reverie.

I shake my head and look up at him. "Hmm…?"

"Where did you go just now?"

I blink a few times and notice that we're already back at the MGM. "I…" I shake my head again. "It's nothing. I just got lost in thought."

He raises an eyebrow. "It's not nothing if you just zoned out like that the whole way back." He squeezes my hand. "Nothing has changed. You can still talk to me. Just because you and I share a last name now doesn't mean things are different."

"But it is, Dane. Can't you see?" I pull my hand away from him and hurry into the hotel. I suddenly feel way beyond exposed.

I dodge a few people in the lobby and beeline to the elevator bank that holds the elevator to our private suite. I don't need to look to know that guards are following me. I've never been more grateful for them. I just feel like I need to be alone. Dane knows me well enough to understand that, and it's one more thing that throws me so much with him. He's so respectful, but is he just fucking with me?

I cross my arms in front of me and try to fade away into the corner of the elevator as a couple of guards step in with me. Just as the doors are about to close, a hand stops them. I look up, startled, as my heart jumps into my throat. I don't know why I expect my thoughts of Thurston to make him manifest in front of me, but I fully believe it will happen. When I see it's Josh standing there, I let out the biggest sigh of relief.

"You scared me," I say softly as he steps inside.

"I could say the same for you. What the hell's going on?" He leans against the elevator wall and looks down at me.

I quickly look at my feet because anything is better than his piercing gaze. "I can't get out of my head. I need a second to just breathe."

"I think you're running away."

My eyes snap to his, and I glare. "What do you really know about me? Huh? Nothing. Except what's on paper."

"Well, that's not true at all. I know your favorite color is pink. I know you hate daffodils with a blinding fucking rage, and if anyone puts the color yellow in front of you, you glare at it like it should be burned at the stake. You're obsessed with Salem Witch Trials. One of your favorite things to do is paint. You think you're really bad at it, but you could probably do your own gallery show. You tell everyone you hate wearing dresses, but you don't. And mostly, I know that at heart, you're what people call a true submissive. You might walk out there and act like a big, tough executive, but you thrive off orders. You feel uncomfortable giving them. When you're home at night, the last thing you want to do is make decisions. It's why you take so well to Dane picking your outfits."

I just stare at him in shock. "How do you possibly know any of that?"

"Part of my job is being observant. Picking up details others miss. I've been around when Dane texts you with his outfit choices, so I know you ask him a lot. I'm not a betting man, but I'd bet all of my billions that he picked the outfit you're wearing right now and the one you wore when you got married earlier."

I nibble my lip and look down again because everything he said is one-hundred percent correct, and now I feel even more exposed. "I just need a few minutes, Josh. I need to breathe."

"No. What you need is Dane. Because what's going on in your mind right now is something that can be easily resolved with a conversation. What you want is to hide because you're used to it. That's how you've always dealt with things until you were forced to stand up and defend yourself."

I'm silent the entire way up to our floor. When the doors open, I make no move to exit. The guards do what they're trained to do, though, and check the hall. They both keep a foot in the way of the doors to keep them from closing. When they look at me, I still don't make a move to exit. I can feel everyone's eyes on me as I sigh.

"You're right... I'm running away."

"I know. So how about we go back down, and you have a conversation with him? And then you do what you had planned because I know you were excited about that."

I nod. "Okay."

Josh puts an arm around me and hugs me tight to his side. I close my eyes and let myself melt slightly as I soak in his never ending strength. "You know it's completely normal for you to feel like you do. Unsure and in need of reassurance. You think you need to constantly be the strong one, but you don't. It's okay to crack under pressure and fall apart."

"It's just that it's too good. He's too good. When is it going to fall apart? When are you all going to realize I'm not good enough or worth your time?"

"First of all, I can assure you that I never waste my time or efforts on someone who isn't worthy of it. You, sweetheart, are. The sooner you realize that not all people in the world are assholes, and that you can count on someone other than yourself or your brother, the better. But I think in order for you to understand that, you first need to see your own worth. You need to take a look at the things you've achieved, the things you've survived, but most importantly, the things that make you who you are. Because until you see that you're good enough for yourself, you'll never be good enough, in your eyes, to anyone else. That was a hard lesson I had to learn. I'm still teaching myself every single day. But it's okay."

I burrow a little further into him, accepting the comfort he's offering. "Tell me what to do."

"Accept who you are, for starters. It's okay to be tough girl in the boardroom. When you're home, you don't need to be. Lay it at Dane's feet. I bet you'll feel pretty comfortable with what it brings you."

I know he's saying I need to accept the submissive side of me. The problem is I blame that side for getting me into the situation I was in. I never want to feel weak like that again. I also know I need to talk to Dane. I just don't know if I can since part of the problem is that I'm falling in love with him and waiting for him to show his true colors. I'm certain they'll be bad.

I need to get out of my head. I've told Dane everything, including all of the things I'd been keeping from him. He hasn't walked away or shunned me.

I let out a breath. "I feel like I'm being tricked. That he's going to flip over a new leaf. Like everyone has. Money, sex, or getting to my boss. That's what everyone wants from me."

"Well, I can assure you Dane has his own money. More than your net worth. I promise. His brother is your boss. So, that's off the table. And he doesn't just want sex. He's not like that. If you took it off the table completely, he'd respect that because he loves you. In three years, it's never been like that with him. Nothing has changed."

I shake my head. "Everything has. Don't you see?"

"No. I don't. I see a guy doing everything he can to protect the woman he loves. Just like he's been doing since he met you. He may have fallen first, but that doesn't mean he's out to get you, Skyla. Dane isn't like that. But the only way you'll learn that and accept it is if you talk to him. Stop putting up walls and just let everything that's happening right now happen." Josh looks at the guards as the doors open. "Not a word of this conversation."

"Goes without saying, sir," one of them responds. It's then I realize that the marriage we've been trying to prove to everyone is not fake has just been exposed to these two men as fake."

I sigh. "I'm terrible at this fake marriage thing."

"Ma'am, if I may," the other guard begins, "you're really not. Up until this point, we didn't know. Our job, though, is to keep you and the family safe. We don't care if the marriage is real or fake. We have orders from our boss, who is the man standing right next to you."

He doesn't know it, but his words actually soothe me slightly. The idea that I'm surrounded by people who truly respect authority is calming.

That feeling doesn't last, though. My mind trails right back to Thurston and how his men also respected authority.

His.

Suddenly, the man I was running from is the very one I need.

I spot Dane leaning against a wall with Taylor standing next to him. His eyes fall on me when I step off the elevator behind the guards. Dane stands to his full height and watches me with so much concern all over his handsome features that I nearly cry.

But it's more than that.

There's something else in his eyes that makes my heart feel like it's not beating anymore. Something that makes his jade eyes darken; his features soften. Something that makes his protective instincts shine through. Something I've never seen in anyone else. Something he's shown me so many times, but I've ignored it all.

Love. Real, true love.

Not that I've never seen love in anyone else. Austin shows it all of the time. I even see it in Josh and Alex and the other guys sometimes. Even from Raleigh and Harleigh, but it's all family type love. Like a sister or something.

It's different with Dane. It's the kind of love that everyone dreams of seeing in their significant other. It catches me so off guard that I barely even notice he's walking towards me until his arms are wrapped around me and he's swaying with me like there's no one else in the world. Just like at the wedding, I feel like I'm somewhere on a private island with him. Like no one else in the world is near us or can see us. It's just us.

"I keep thinking that you're somehow going to turn into the bad guy," I whisper.

"Never happening. I don't care how many times I need to say that. I don't care what I have to do to prove it to you. I'll do it," he whispers back.

"Why do I keep going back and forth? One second, you're the good guy. The next, you're going to destroy me."

"PTSD works in fucked up ways. And it's something you're going to deal with for days, months, years, but I'm not going anywhere. I'm not. You're not in this alone anymore. I've made mistakes. I've allowed you to think I wasn't coming back. I've walked away because you asked me when I should've stayed. I'll regret that for the rest of my life." He tightens his grip. "Baby, I'm not going anywhere. Lesson learned. The only reason I didn't follow you is because Ryan held me back while Josh followed. And I trusted that Josh would say to you what I couldn't."

I sniffle. "I'm really sorry. I got overwhelmed."

"Don't be. Never apologize for getting overwhelmed. Next time, just talk to me. Let me help you." He pulls back slightly and kisses my forehead softly. "What do you say to a Fat Tuesday?"

I blink at him in shock. "A... what...?"

He grins. "You can't come to Vegas without indulging in a Fat Tuesday. It's life changing." He takes my hand and tugs me with him. I can't help but laugh at his excitement as he leads me to an escalator.

Minutes later, we both have giant blue drinks in our hands. "How... big is this?"

"You don't want to know. Just trust me." Dane grins as he sucks some through a straw.

I eye it. "It's honestly as long as my entire torso. Like from my waist to my neck."

"Mmhmm. Try it."

I crinkle my nose before taking a small sip. He refused to tell me what's in the monstrosity of a drink. He really wants it to be a surprise.

As soon as the frozen liquid hits my tongue, it explodes into a multitude of flavorful goodness that would send me to my knees if I wasn't already sitting down. My eyes roll back in my head, and I moan in ecstasy.

"Oh my God. It's better than an orgasm."

Dane cracks up. "If you really think that, I'm not doing my job."

I blush and giggle. "You might need to step up your game after this."

"I'm taking that as a challenge. And it's accepted."

I smile and hide behind the giant plastic cup. "Can we play in the casino a little? I saw this slot machine when we walked through earlier that I want to try. It looked fun."

"The Michael Jackson one?"

"That one and the Britney Spears one. And there was this True Blood one that looked like a blast. I saw someone in the bonus round on that, and she was leaping up and down."

Dane laughs. "Anything you want."

I squeak and hop off the bench we snagged. Dane sticks close to me and drops his arm around my waist as we head to the casino. As soon as I feel his fingertips grip my hip, it's like all of the bad things that have been messing with my head fade away. As each second goes by, he makes me feel more and more comfortable.

While I play the machines I was excited about late into the night, Dane never leaves my side. He does little things to comfort me right when I need it. I don't know if he can sense the slight shift or anxiousness or something, but it doesn't matter because by the end of the night, I'm so used to it that I don't even realize it's happening.

The only things I'm really thinking about are I'm having fun, and the only person I've truly let go with like this is Dane.

Those two thoughts are enough for me to let a little bit more of my fortified wall down...

Chapter Eleven

🐚 Dane 🐚

(Two Weeks Later)

I look up at a knock on my office door. "Yeah," I bark as I drop my eyes back down to the report in front of me.

"I have something I think you'd like to see, sir."

I smile a half-smile as I look back up. "Aimee. We've talked about this. You don't need to call me 'sir'."

The slender, raven-haired woman in front of me widens her eyes almost comically. She sets a sheet of paper in front of me and stands in front of my desk biting her lip. "I saw this come across. It was sent to Lieutenant Reddick as well."

It's then I realize it's not that she forgets she doesn't need to call me 'sir'. It's that she is quite literally not capable of doing it. "How about you call me, Lieutenant? Does that make you feel a little better?"

She smiles brightly. Her short bob moves as she nods enthusiastically. Considering the tough, take no shit cop that Aimee is, I never would've pegged her for the type of woman who submits completely to authority like that. She can't call me by my first name because it's not comfortable for her. I'm just sorry it's taken me nearly two years of working with her to realize it. I should've.

Aimee transferred to my team from our Major Crimes division. I took note of her exemplary work and poached her, more or less. It was one of the best decisions I've ever made. She's just as good about solving crimes as she is kicking in doors and taking down bad guys. She's been a good asset to me and my small team.

Other than Aimee and Cole, my Sergeant, I have two other detectives. Aiden and Lucas both came from SWAT, but they also worked in our special victims division. That unit investigates sex crimes from kids to the elderly and everything in between. It's a mentally taxing job, and while they loved what they did, they were happy to get out. Given their track record, I was happy to take them.

Since I set my team up around four years ago now, it's been me, Cole, Aiden, and Lucas. We got a little busier, so I requested and got approved for one more person. Aimee was a no brainer. We'd worked with her on a few cases, and I couldn't have been more impressed.

I look at what she brought me. "So, what am I looking at?"

"An arrest warrant for Thurston Maxwell, sir."

My eyebrows shoot up, and I look a little closer. "No shit. They got enough to haul him in from the fire?"

"Not just enough. They basically proved he's the one who did it. Security footage from other buildings has him all over that area. We have footage from a business right next to the pizza place that directly links him at that location that very night. It shows him sneaking in the backdoor with the very bomb we found. It wasn't covered up at all. It was like he wanted to be caught."

I drum fingers on my desk as I study the warrant. After a few moments, I zero in on the address listed. "Why is this address not his penthouse in New York? And why does this address sound familiar?"

"That's exactly what I thought. So, I looked it up, then immediately called Taylor."

"Oh, holy shit." I lean back in my chair with my mouth half open.

"Yep. It's Chase Shaw's old estate."

"I thought he still owned it."

"It's listed for sale. That's why I called Taylor. He's coming down. He said he had to call Chase."

"Motherfucker, this can't be happening. He's either using this address to start a fucking war, or he really bought it, and Chase doesn't have a fucking clue who it was sold to."

"I'm betting on the second one. I don't think he's stupid enough to start a war. Just like I don't think he's stupid enough to actually be in plainview of cameras with the very bomb he planned to use to blow up a pizzeria."

"The same one I frequent."

"It was targeted. It had to have been. He's after Skyla and going through you to get to her. If he can get to you by targeting things you love, he thinks it will break you more and more until the walls you've built around her crumble."

I glare. "Like fucking hell."

Taylor picks that moment to glide into my office and slam the door behind him. Aimee nearly jumps over my desk into my arms, and I turn my glare to Taylor.

"Might I suggest you find it before I bring the entire department down on you!" Taylor barks into his phone before hanging up.

I soften my sharp gaze when I look back at Aimee. "Go grab the team," I say calmly.

She's fierce as hell when we're out on missions, but when she's in office, she hates yelling or any kind of drama. I can't count how many times I've let her sit in here to relax and collect herself when things have gotten hectic in the bullpen.

Aimee scurries out of my office with a nod.

I turn that steely gaze back to Taylor. "Would you stop scaring my fucking detectives?"

He glances at the door. "I still say she's getting her ass kicked at home."

"I've seen no evidence of that. She's submissive to authority. That I can tell you." His words do make me wonder more than I had before, though. I'll have to pay more attention.

"All I'm saying is something is happening with her."

Before I can respond, Cole leads Aimee, Aiden, and Lucas into my office. When I got my office, I splurged a little bit and bought some pretty comfortable furniture. I have some brown leather arm chairs and a nice couch to match that I've spent more than one night sleeping on.

Everyone settles, but I very suddenly notice the difference in Aimee. She's usually smiling and pretty happy. She has a favorite chair near the window, but she's nearly dived into the one closest to my desk. The one Cole usually goes for. It's easiest for me to hand him stuff if I need to during team meetings.

Cole pauses and raises an eyebrow. Aimee's eyes shift to the floor as she crosses her arms across her middle section. Apparently, it's not only alarming for me. All eyes shift to her then me. I give a slight shake of my head to tell them all to leave it and say nothing. I'm on complete alert now. This is more than just her being submissive to authority. Something is very, very wrong. This behavior has gone from normal to abnormal faster than I can blink.

It's not the first time Taylor has mentioned things to me about her behavior. She's a model cop. I thought she just hated arguing or loud noises or something. I thought she preferred a more quiet environment to concentrate, but now, I'm wondering if Taylor was right. If he's been seeing shit I haven't.

I glance at Taylor as he sits in front of me next to Cole, who also chose to sit in front of my desk. "Tell me what Chase said," I say.

"That he sold through a realtor. He said he looked through the offer. It was more than what he asked for and the highest of the seven that was brought to him. He took it, but he said the name wasn't Thurston Maxwell. He pulled out the paperwork from sale. It was Graham Thurswell."

"That has to be an alias," I rumble as I look down at the arrest warrant.

"It's his middle name," Aimee says to me with a small shrug as she nods to the arrest warrant.

I glance down and see it. I don't know why I didn't put two and two together before. I must really be tired. "An alias is looking more and more plausible."

"Lieutenant Reddick," Taylor says into his ringing phone when he answers. All of our eyes are on him. "See? Not so hard, was it? And you even avoided a search warrant. I'll be there in ten minutes to pick it up." He hangs up. "The realtor grabbed a copy of the sale agreement for me. I'll grab a copy from Chase to compare. The name, though, is Graham M. Thurswell."

"That can't be a coincidence," Aimee says. "We should grab him right now. I'll grab my gear."

"Not yet, slugger," I say with a chuckle that's very much forced. "We have some investigating to do. You know we don't hurry things. We do it right from the start. Less chance of a fuck up that way."

She visibly slumps, but keeps up the facade of eager detective. "Sorry, Lieutenant." She looks at her watch with a sigh.

I shoot everyone a look that tells them to stay right where they are as I clear my throat. "Hot date?" I ask teasingly.

She rolls her eyes and laughs. "Yes. With my cat. He's probably starving by this point and plotting my demise for being late with his Frisky dinner. The last time I was late, he decided he wasn't sleeping in bed with me and refused all snuggles. He even stuck his nose up at the tuna fish I tried to bribe him with."

"Well, man. You should probably get home. We'll reconvene tomorrow and discuss our plan."

"Thank you, Lieutenant. I'm tired anyway. Didn't sleep well." She smiles and nearly bolts to the door. She doesn't look back as she flies through it and quickly starts gathering her stuff from her desk.

"Aiden and Lucas. Follow her. Report to me where she goes. Cole, go with Taylor. Go over the sales report with him. Find the differences. The hesitation to give it to him has me on edge. I don't like it."

"What are you sensing?" Taylor asks as soon as Cole, Aiden, and Lucas all leave the office looking as if they're getting ready to go home as well.

"Same thing you are. Guarantee it."

"You think her boyfriend is Thurston?"

"Yep. And that her excitement with getting him now is her way of getting out of a fucked up situation that she's obviously scared to death to be a part of."

"You're on the track I am. If she goes to him, call me. I'll grab my team. We'll go together."

"I have half a fucking mind to call Ryan and Josh."

"Me too. But wait and see where she goes first. Last thing we want to do is jump when there's no fire."

"Ready to go, Taylor?" Cole asks.

Taylor glances at the clock on my wall. "I'll send a patrol officer," he says. "Got a bad feeling." He starts texting as Cole sits in his usual chair after closing my door.

"You know, if this is what we're thinking, this is a huge problem. Our team got some very sensitive information regarding Skyla and this case," Cole says.

I glance at Taylor. "Yeah, Taylor thinks she's in a relationship with him. And that it's like Skyla's. The more and more I think about it, the more I think it's completely true. She's submissive to authority. She has been for a long time, even before she joined our team, but this is another level."

"I've noticed some interesting behaviors myself, but I've never seen bruises or anything. She's always played being jumpy as being tired. We all get that way, so I didn't think a lot of it," Cole says.

"It's way more than that," Taylor pipes in. "She's jumpy and everything, yes, but when she's going to be later than the usual time she leaves, she always takes off to the bathroom. And every time she comes out, she's wiping her eyes like she's been crying. When she comes in the next day, she's stiff. Sore. I've never seen bruises either, but the other behaviors are just becoming more and more frequent."

I tap the pen I'm holding against my thigh. "Skyla said he never left bruises where people could see them. And if he did, she'd wear makeup to cover it. She'd have to wear more, but it covered it up. That's all she cared about."

Cole nods. "She's been wearing darker makeup. Darker lipstick. Not the natural kind she usually does. She was wearing purple lipstick today."

I pick up my cellphone and call Josh. Just as it starts ringing, my caller ID shows another incoming call from Aiden. I know if I don't answer, he'll immediately call Cole.

"Dane. What can I do for you?"

"We have a problem," I begin. I don't wait for him to respond. "It's Aimee." Josh knows all of my team members. He helped me vet them. He has to. We need to be sure in the beginning that my team knows what they're getting into; that they'll be working with the mafia.

"What about her?" His voice has lowered to a far more dangerous level. I already know he's glaring at something hard enough that it might burst into flames.

"We think she's in a relationship with Thurston. Before you freak out on me, though, just hear me out. We've noticed a few things here and there that might signify abuse, but she's good at playing things off. Me, Cole, and Taylor are all sitting here pinpointing small things we've noticed, and they all add up. Today, though, we found some shit out I was going to tell you about as soon as I got my team mobilized. We have an arrest warrant for Thurston. We're going to need backup, just to be on the safe side. We don't know how big the fuckers have gotten again. Aimee is the one who gave it to me. She was pretty happy and bubbly until Taylor slammed my office door. It freaked her out. She almost jumped over my desk into my lap."

"That sounds zero percent like Aimee."

"Yeah. That's what I thought. Anyway, I had her grab the team. She sits next to the window when we have team meetings. Religiously. Today she sat where Cole does, which is next to my desk so I can pass things to him easily."

"We're getting into negative numbers at this point. It's so unlike her."

"Yep. It gets worse. She knows we research. Investigate. We observe. We mobilize. She wanted to go after him right now. Like grabbing her gear, let's fucking go, kind of right now. No plan. Nothing. When I stopped her and told her we need to do a few things before we go after him, she visibility deflated. Like she couldn't stand the thought of not getting him this very second."

"She's heading towards the mansion Code Three," Cole says when he hangs up.

It's all any of us need to jump into action. "We also found out Thurston bought Chase's mansion under a false name. We were about to start on proving it and doing some observation," I say as I follow Taylor and Cole. "Before she left, she was pretty impatient. She was looking at her watch and talking about how she needs to feed her cat." I pause. "She doesn't have a cat. She hates them. It was like she was speaking in code, but I don't know why. I don't know why she didn't just tell us."

"She made them," Cole says as I jump in his truck next to him. Taylor gets in his own truck and follows us as Cole takes the lead.

"I'm putting you on speaker, Josh," I say. "That's all I know right now other than when she left, I had Aiden and Lucas follow."

"Okay. I'm mobilizing a team. We're on the way."

Cole puts his phone on speaker and hands it to me as he drives. "She took an unmarked squad without authorization instead of her personal vehicle. Aiden thinks she made them and took off with lights and sirens. They're still following."

"Sounds to me like she knows exactly what she's doing," Josh says.

"She just pulled into the driveway. Didn't close the gates. Gates were left open," Aiden says.

"Stay out," Josh commands, reading my mind. "This is either a trap, or a cry for help. Observe her."

"Yes, sir. She's stepping out of the car now and looking around."

I look at Cole as my heart starts racing. "I don't fucking like this."

"Not one bit." Cole steps on the gas and flips his own lights and sirens on. I have them on my personal vehicle as he does. Taylor and Nick have them, too. It's in case we get woken up in the middle of the night and need to get somewhere fast.

"Have someone call Taylor," I say to Josh. "He's behind us. No idea what's going on."

"I'll take care of it," Josh says.

"She's walking inside with her head down, but she made direct eye contact with Lucas," Aiden says. "She's giving us a Code Four signal."

And that's when my heart drops into my stomach. "Where is her hand?"

"Behind her back," Aiden says. "Lucas agrees with me. She's not okay."

"You're right. We're on the way. Bringing backup. Follow her. Be careful. If she held her hand up and did that like she does on a call or something, she'd be signaling to you that she's okay. Her hand behind her back like that or in any other way that looks like she's trying to hide what she's doing is a sign for domestic abuse or a call for help."

"Oh shit," Lucas says. I hear car doors opening.

"We're going in," Aiden says.

96

"We're a couple minutes out," Cole says.

"Yes sir." Aiden hangs up.

"Jesus Christ," I rumble.

A few minutes later, Cole skids to a stop in the driveway behind the squad Aimee took, and we don't like what we see at all. We both take our guns out as we jump out of the truck. Taylor follows close behind.

We run as silently as we can along the house to the front door that's been kicked open. Our heads are on a swivel. It's not long after that, we see several black SUVs. They all come to a stop in the driveway and along the road. A lot of people with guns jump out. I've never been happier to see anyone. With silent commands from Josh, who is running to us, his teams take positions around the house.

Josh positions himself in front of me. Taylor is behind me. Cole is behind him. Josh keeps his hand up to keep us quiet. I'm sure he's listening to everyone barking in his ear over his earpiece. When I'm about to lose my mind at how fucking quiet it is in the house, Josh starts counting down quietly. As soon as the word 'enter' leaves his mouth, chaos ensues.

All of us follow him into the house, guns drawn. Guards bust down doors around the house. We're all moving, but there's absolutely no sounds other than us. I'm becoming more and more apprehensive the further we get in the house. I've seen no one but us and Josh's team.

"Oh my fucking hell," Taylor says.

My eyes snap to him. I'm suddenly filled with both dread and anger all at once. "Fuck!" I burst out because I can't help it.

Trusting Josh and his team to take care of me and my guys, I rush to Aimee. She's lying on the floor on top of busted glass from the coffee table she obviously went through. I reach down and start feeling for a pulse. I let out a breath I didn't know I was holding when I feel one. It's faint, but it's there.

I look up at Cole. He's kneeling over Aiden, who's slumped against a wall with a nasty as fuck blood stain trailing down it. Cole is checking for injuries while making sure he's still breathing.

Fuck, please let him still be breathing.

Cole nods, visibly relieved. "Pulse is strong."

"We need medical," Taylor says. He's kneeling next to Lucas, who's sprawled out in the entryway to a long hallway. "He's good, but they need to be checked out. Especially her." He nods to Aimee.

"Watch him," Cole says to a guard. I look back at him as the guard kneels next to Aiden and Taylor calls EMS. I watch Cole walk towards Josh.

I furrow my eyebrows. "What's going on?" I ask. Josh looks like he's frozen. If I didn't know better, I'd swear he'd been shot and just hasn't fallen yet.

His eyes are wide.

He looks white as a ghost.

His gun is dangling from his finger like he's about to drop it.

And his gaze is fixed on Aimee…

Chapter Twelve

☙ Skyla ❧

I worriedly get the ice water Cole asked for and hurry back to Josh's office where he is. Cole takes it as I chew my lip and sniffle. He opens the door just enough to slip inside. My eyes can't help but follow him. I briefly see Josh lying on his couch with Jessa lying on top of him running her fingers through his hair before Cole closes the door.

A few hours ago, Cole brought Josh home. Dane texted me, told me to grab Alex and get to Josh's immediately. He gave very little details. He only said that Josh needs support right now, and that he'd be going to the hospital. He said he was okay, but three of his team members needed to go. I've been worried about him, them, and Josh ever since.

I slide down the wall until I'm sitting on the floor and wrap my arms around my knees. "Is he okay? What's happening?" I wipe my eyes not understanding in the slightest why I'm so overly emotional all of the sudden. I'm probably about to start my period.

Alex sits down across from me with his back against the wall. "He will be."

"I mean, I know about Jessa and everything that happened, but..." I trail off and focus on my fingers.

He nods. "Seeing Aimee lying in glass like that brought up memories of Jessa. Josh is a really put together person. Tough. But even the toughest have vulnerabilities. Sometimes, Josh can't sleep at night. The flashbacks and memories of shit he's been through just don't leave him alone."

I sniffle. "Josh is one of the greatest men I've ever met. I hate this is happening."

"I admit, this hasn't happened in a long time. But with this kind of stuff, it comes out of nowhere. Josh is one of the lucky ones. He has a good team and even better family who love and support him. When he comes out of this, he'll talk to Lyric. By the time you wake up tomorrow, he'll be the same loveable asshole we all care so much about."

I chuckle a little bit. "I wish I could just hug him. It sucks so bad when flashbacks happen."

Alex chuckles and shows me his phone. "See? Lyric said to let her at all the past memories so she can beat them up. And a promise that sounds like a threat that I have to show him this message to make him laugh or else." He chuckles again. "Josh has a good support system. Even from people who are far away."

I chuckle a little more. "Still, I know it's hard when flashbacks come at you like that."

"Well, the good thing is that Jessa is in there right now assuring him that all of the shit that happened before wasn't his fault. It's hard to be at fault for something when you're being drugged and controlled like he was. I still have a lot of guilt about not seeing it. So do Gavin and Damon. Lance would, but he didn't know Josh before all of the shit went down. Trust me, though, when I say that Josh is getting everything he needs right now. He needs Jessa to assure him that she's okay because he wasn't seeing Aimee on that floor. He was seeing her."

I nod understanding fully what he was seeing. I've seen a little bit of blood from cutting my leg while shaving, and suddenly, I was transported right back to cleaning myself up after he'd cut my lip by biting it while he was kissing me.

I sigh. "I just hope he's okay."

Alex leans over and pats my knee. "Trust me. No one here is going to stand by and let him not be okay."

I nod. "It's just that… I've… gotten so close to everyone. I feel a little bit like it's my own brother who is dealing with this."

"I understand. Believe me. Best way to combat it is do something else. Distract yourself."

I chew the inside of my cheek while Cole sits next to me after coming back out of the room. After a few minutes of silence, I finally make a decision. "I think I'm going to cook. I'm not the best at it, but I can do a mean flatbread pizza."

"One of Josh's favorites," Cole says with a grin. "Put spinach on there, he'll be your best friend."

For the first time in hours, my smile is bright. I nod as I get up, fully committed to making the best flatbread pizza Josh has ever had. He's a really good cook, though, so I'm not going to try to beat him. Maybe the second best he's ever had instead.

I'm grateful to find everything I need for a couple of pizzas and set to work making them. Tomatoes and spinach with some feta cheese sounds amazing to me, so I make that for one of the pizzas. I decide to put some onions on it and make it with garlic sauce. I make another one with spinach, mushrooms, and tomatoes with black olives. I add some salt and pepper to the top.

As I wait for them to bake, I take out my phone and call Dane. I fight tears as I anxiously hold on as his phone rings. When it gets to the fourth ring, though, a tear spills. I don't know why, but I need to hear his voice right now.

"Hey, baby. We're just heading out now. I have Aimee with me. The guys are gonna stay with Cole for a couple days. Just want to be cautious. You okay? How's Josh?"

My heart skips a beat at his voice and him calling me 'baby'. I love when he says that. Or when he uses other pet names for me. Honey. Sweetheart. Sky.

"I'm… dealing… I feel so bad for Josh right now. I probably wasn't supposed to see, but he's lying on the couch in his office with Jessa right now. Alex said he'll be okay, but I guess I don't really know right now how he is."

"I'm betting he's doing a lot better than he was. And I'm sure by the time I get there, he'll be his usual bossy self. My little brother has more inner strength than he realizes."

I nod slowly and sigh. "I hope so…"

"What else is going on? I can hear it in your voice."

I sigh again. "You know me too well. This is a problem."

He chuckles. "Tell me, beautiful."

"It's just that… I don't know. I guess I feel there's more than what Cole told me."

"There is, baby. And I'm sorry, but that's my fault. I want to be the one to tell you. I know it's going to upset you, and I need to be the one there to catch you when you fall. I know that doesn't help with the anxiety of knowing something bigger went down, but I promise I'm almost there. I'll tell you everything."

"I -" I cut myself off and bite my tongue, the words I was about to say dying on my lips. "I can't wait until you're back. Will Aimee be staying with us then?"

"Well, that's something I wanted to talk to you about. We're pulling through the gate now, sweet girl."

"Okay. I'll see you soon." I turn and start making more pizzas as soon as Dane hangs up.

"There's some breadsticks in the freezer," a deep voice rumbles just as I'm starting to put some toppings on the last pizza.

I look up and see Josh. I feel like I drop from the most anxious high I've ever been on straight to the pits of relief. "Oh my God, Josh. Are you okay?"

"Took me a while. But yeah, I'm okay." He walks around the counter and gives me a side hug. He turns and pulls breadsticks out of the freezer. "I made these a few days ago. Thought they'd be good for those middle of the nights when I want a snack and a book."

"One of my favorite things about you is that you enjoy books. I wish I could read more. I love just curling up with a classic and losing myself sometimes."

He chuckles and pulls something else out from a cupboard. He plugs it in as I tilt my head. "It's a warmer. I use it when I'm making food for everyone. It keeps everything crispy and perfect. At least for the amount of time I need it to. Any longer than maybe thirty minutes, and it gets either too soggy or too hard."

"That's a brilliant idea."

"I've learned a few things over the years." He turns back to me and starts setting the breadsticks on a pan. He melts some butter and adds garlic to it as I finish adding the pepperoni to the pizza. I put it in the oven with another of the pizzas after pulling out the first two. Josh puts the breadsticks in and sets the pizza I just took out in the warmer. "So, how are things going with Dane?"

I blush and hide behind my hair. "Okay. He's been good about keeping things like they were. The only difference is that when I get too close, he doesn't let me run away. It's really weird, though. Being married to someone I wasn't even dating."

Josh leans against the counter. "I can see how that would be difficult. I think you wanted to be, though. I know he did."

I chuckle. "He's so far out of my league. Guys like him just don't fall for girls like me."

"Are you talking about smart, beautiful women who are successful, strong, and sweet? Because that's how he sees you. We're all lucky to know you. Not just him."

I hug myself. "I appreciate that. I don't know if I believe it, but I do appreciate it."

"Maybe you should start believing it."

I turn quickly. Dane is leaning against the doorframe to the kitchen. Those pesky tears prick my eyes again, and I run to him before I can stop myself from doing something so foolish. In my mind, he picks me up like in a Hallmark love story. He spins me around and kisses me so sweetly, but I feel everything. All the love and passion he holds flows into me and warms my soul.

So, when I feel him lift me, my legs wrap around his waist just as automatically as my arms wrap around his neck. Just like in my mini fantasy, Dane's lips meet mine in a kiss right from the most sugary romance movie imaginable. But I don't care because I'm consumed with the sparks and feelings behind it that make me feel like I could burst into a firework of multiple colors.

I feel my cheeks get wet. It's like some kind of block has been demolished. I let the tears fall. I feel so much closer to Dane so suddenly that my head is spinning. Instead of feeling like I want to run far away, though, I hug him tighter because I don't ever want to let him go. While the thought scares me, I find the immense level of love I feel for him is far more intense than anything else.

"Where is this coming from?" he rumbles deeply against my neck right before he kisses it.

"Maybe it was the thought of you being hurt," I whisper. "Or maybe it was seeing Josh like that. Maybe it was seeing the way Jessa helped him through. Maybe it's knowing Aimee has no one to help her right now. That Aiden and Lucas don't. All I know is I don't want to lose you. I love you, and I don't ever want to let you go. I need you in my life, but what's so much more than that is that I want you to be. I want you to be here always, and I want to be with you always. I don't want this to be fake anymore. I just want everything to be real."

"It is real, baby. Everything is real. A piece of paper and the need to put a ring on your finger as a type of claim so your asshole ex shows up and lets us give him everything that's coming to him means fuck all." He keeps his lips pressed against my neck and sways back and forth with me in his arms. "If you want this to be forever, then it'll be just that, but don't think it's not real. We can have a big reception. We can do a big wedding and say the vows over again. I'll marry you every day if that's what you want."

"It's so fast. We weren't even really together when we did this."

"In my eyes, you've been the only one since I first met you, Sky. Being with you, no matter what capacity it is, is the happiest I've ever been. There is no one else out there for me. I know what I want. You. I want you."

I sniffle and keep my face buried in his shoulder. I vaguely feel him moving to let Josh by with the pizza.

"Stay married to me..."

"There's nothing I'd like more than to stay married to you, baby," he whispers with such conviction that I can't help but melt into him.

For the first time since I ran from Thurston, I feel something other than fear.

Hope.

Chapter Thirteen

☙ Dane ☙

"You gonna be okay?" I ask Aimee as I lean against the doorframe of the guest bedroom. "Do those clothes fit okay?"

Aimee nods a little weakly. "Yes, Lieutenant. I'm just really sore. Can you say thank you for me to Skyla for the stuff she's letting me use?" She sits on the edge of the bed.

"I can. How are you doing otherwise?"

She's silent for so long that I actually move towards her. I sit on the edge of the bed, and that seems to be all it takes for her to burst into tears. "I'm so sorry! I could've stopped this so long ago! I knew who he -"

"Stop, Aimee." I pull her into my side and hug her as she sobs. "You were scared. You and I have worked on so many cases together over the past few years. You know as well as I do that fear plays a huge factor in things like this. You can't play the blame game like this. You had to think of yourself. The only mistake you made, Aimee, was not trusting me enough to come to me and tell me, but I can't even be upset with you for that. You had no idea how everything would come back to you. You were in survival mode. Truth is, you did what you thought was best. It wasn't the greatest idea, but it got you out."

"It got us all hurt!" she shrieks as she tries to move. I see Skyla appear in the doorway worriedly as I hug Aimee tighter.

"Survival mode. You have to remember that. You did what you thought was best. You got help. You made deliberate decisions to get help. You knew I'd have some follow you. You had a backup plan just in case I didn't by taking a squad you weren't authorized to take. I don't ever want there to be a next time, but if you're ever in trouble, you can come to me. You know I'll do what needs to be done. This situation proved it, right?"

It takes her a few minutes to calm down enough to nod, but I know she's beating herself up. She's similar to Skyla in a lot of ways, but she has Thurston in common with her. I motion for Skyla to come in as I hug Aimee even tighter.

Without being directed, Skyla sits down on the other side of Aimee and hugs her. She starts whispering to her as she rocks her back and forth. Whatever she's saying works well enough to get Aimee to release me and cry into Skyla's shoulder as she grips Skyla's shirt.

I hear bits and pieces of what she's whispering. Things like 'you're a fighter' and 'you're capable'. She tells her that she can pull through, and she's wiser and braver for all she went through. It's pretty obvious to me that Aimee needs Skyla's support right now, so I quietly make my exit.

I walk down the stairs to the kitchen to make tea. I've learned a few things from my British little sister. Lyric says anything can be solved with tea and good conversation. Even if it's with the voices in our head.

After talking to Aimee, Lucas, and Aiden, I found out that as soon as Aimee closed the door to the mansion and took off her gun, as she was demanded to do, Thurston was all over her. He was yelling, screaming, and throwing her against things. Aimee didn't lock the door. She only pretended to, and Thurston was cocky enough to trust that she'd listen to him.

Aimee, however, knew help was on the other side of the door. Lucas and Aiden busted through with their guns raised. They didn't expect Thurston would have someone with him. They didn't know who it was, but they saw he was dressed in leather and had a patch on his jacket. They couldn't make out what it was before they were in a fight for their lives.

A fight they lost quickly as soon as Aimee was thrown through a table after being beaten to within inches of her life. They'd been disarmed quickly by what they described as a damn ninja with skills they'd never come across.

As soon as they told me that, I knew the fact that they weren't all three dead meant it was a message for me. He's showing me how easy it could be to take things dear to me. How easy it would be to take Skyla from me.

Only, it's not easy. If it was, he'd have done it already. Skyla is well protected. Until this is over, so is my team. They won't be going back to their homes. He's playing a dangerous game that I've gotten too good at over the years.

When the tea I'm making finishes, I bring the two cups upstairs. When I reach Aimee's bedroom, Skyla is still whispering to her, but she's calmed Aimee down considerably. I set the tea on the dresser next to the bed and decide a shower is very much needed. It's one of the most relaxing things I can do after the type of day I've had.

When I finish my shower and dry off, I wrap a towel around my waist and walk out to my bedroom. Skyla is sitting on the edge of the bed, but she looks the most melancholy I've ever seen her. She's hugging herself and looking down at the floor.

"Skyla, baby, what's wrong?" I ask softly as I sit down next to her.

She sniffles and shakes her head. "So much stuff that happened to her. It was all the same." She plays with her fingers as I wait for her to continue. "She tried to tell so many times but chickened out because she was afraid. It was the same as me. She was with him for a little over two years. He was living in a penthouse for a while. She said he just moved into the house not long ago. She thought it was a lot bigger. More places to hide for her, but it didn't work like that. It only got worse."

I slip my arm around her and pull her close. I've already told her everything that happened and all I knew about Thurston. I knew she'd talk to Aimee eventually. I didn't expect it to be tonight, but I'm sure something was calling her to help in that exact moment. I'm sure it was something Aimee needed. I don't blame her. Having someone to talk to who has been through it must be a huge relief.

"Well, the good thing is she helped us get her out, right? It wasn't exactly the most orthodox thing, but we know why she did that. She's safe now. She's okay. She's going to be able to heal in peace."

Skyla nods as she wipes her eyes. "It just… Today… It all made me really feel like I'm so lucky. I have such a great family, and the man of my dreams. I'm wasting it. I'm wasting it all, and I don't want to." She turns to me with red-rimmed eyes, but it's what's behind them that takes my breath away.

I don't have time to fully process what's happening before I'm flat on my back with her wrapped around me. She kisses me with a fervor that takes my breath away. I tangle my fingers in her hair and deepen the kiss even more.

She nips at my tongue and lower lip. She scratches at my shoulders and rubs herself against my rapidly hardening cock. She pulls away and pulls her shirt over her head, not wanting to mess with the buttons. I'd love nothing more than to rip her clothes off and take her right here and now, but watching her do it slams every ounce of control I'd briefly lost right back into me.

"Hey… hey, baby," I grip her hips and stop her from grinding against me as I sit up. She looks at me with wide eyes like she did something wrong and pauses in the middle of taking her bra off. I smooth her hair out of her face. "What are you doing?"

She tries to look down, but I don't let her. She nibbles her lower lip, so I run my thumb over it. Finally, she takes a deep breath. "I'm sorry. I shouldn't have assumed you want me…"

I give her an amused half smile. "Wanting you isn't a question. But you know I'm not taking you unless I know for sure it's what you want. You wanted to take this slow. And I agreed because I love you, baby." I lean in and kiss her softly. "Now, you know I'll give you everything you want, but think about if this is what you want, sweet girl."

She watches me for way too long before she finally shoves away the war of emotions going on behind her pretty eyes. She hits my lips with hers and starts kissing me again. It's all I need from her to know she's ready.

I growl possessively and unhook her bra as I give her the intensity she wants. I slide my tongue into hers and start a Paso Doble. I toss her bra and grip her ass so I can flip her on her back. I straddle her and lean down, taking her nipple in my mouth. I suck hard with a low rumble while I unbutton her slacks. I tug them down as I kiss down her body. When I reach her pussy, I lick while I pull them and her panties off the rest of the way.

"Dane!" Skyla jerks her hips into me like my tongue shocked her.

"My girl likes that, I see." I give her a wicked grin and wink as I pull my towel off and toss it wherever her pants went. I dive back into her pussy with my tongue and move it in a furious, tornadic circle.

"Oh!" Skyla breathes heavily.

I slide one finger inside her and thrust hard, deep, and fast as I crook it against her spot. Her fingers spear my hair as she moans and moves with my thrusts. I lick, nip, and suck my way up to her clit. The second I reach it, I suck it into my mouth and flick it rapidly with my tongue while I fuck her pussy with my finger.

"Mmm…," I moan against her clit.

"Oh… fuck… yes!"

I smile at the desired effect of my voice rumbling against her. Her pussy gets wetter for me and pulses uncontrollably. She closes her legs around my head and pulls me closer to her until my face is buried in her.

Right where I like to be. Her taste is exquisite, unique; unlike anything I've ever enjoyed before, and I can't get enough. Each time I have the honor of having my face between her thighs, I just want to stay longer and longer.

"Dane! I'm… I can't!" She writhes underneath me, bucking her hips into my face.

I nip her clit, making her scream. "Come for me, pretty girl. Give me what I want."

Her thighs start trembling. Her pussy clamps hard around my finger. Instead of thrusting, I keep crooking my finger against her spot as I ravish her clit.

Her hips arch off the bed. "Dane!" she shouts. I'd be concerned about Aimee hearing us, but there are several advantages of being the brother of a mafia king.

Soundproof walls are a thing. I've never been so thankful for them as I am in this moment.

As she's coming down, I slide my hands up her sides, rubbing soothingly to help her relax. I kiss up her body until I reach her nipples. I lick and suck them both, giving them the attention they deserve.

The second she starts writhing and arching again, I lick my way up to her lips. I take them with mine in a kiss that's both gentle and bruising. At the same moment she wraps her legs around my waist, I push my throbbing cock deep inside her, burying myself to the hilt

"Oh, fuck! Dane! So big. So, so big…" Her eyes roll back in her head. Her tight pussy pulses around me, and all I can do as she stretches so prettily around my length is drop my head and bury my face in her neck.

"Christ, you feel like heaven around me." It's everything I fantasized about and more. Hearing her soft moans and whimpers as I fill her is like music to my ears, but staying still is almost torture.

As we both hold each other close, I start to move just enough to relieve some of the ache in my cock. She breathes against my shoulder and runs her fingernails slowly up and down my back. I kiss her neck and pump just a little faster. I pull out a little more with each thrust and push back into her as deep as I can.

"Dane," she whispers.

I kiss up to her lips once more. She closes her eyes, and I passionately and dominantly make her sweet, delectable lips mine. Each thrust makes her wetter. Every time I slide inside her, her pussy seems to suck me in deeper, like I belong there and am never supposed to leave.

Not like I want to. If Little Dane could talk, he'd be telling me all about how he found his new home. How warm it is. How tight and good it feels. How he just wants to burrow inside her and never come out.

"Oh fuck, yes," I rumble against her pretty throat the second I reach it.

"Dane… Yes… Oh, yes!" She digs her heels into my ass like she's spurring a horse. I smile against her throat and thrust faster, harder, and as deep as I can possibly go.

I reach down and grip her ass. I pull her up and into each and every thrust and roll of my hips. I shift just enough to angle my dick so it slides over her clit each time I pound it inside her. Her fingernails dig into my shoulders as her sweet walls start to collapse. Her thighs tremble, and all I want is to feel how good she feels when she's squeezing my cock while she comes.

"Ready to come for me, my beautiful wife?" I glance up just in time to see her flushed cheeks brighten even more as she blushes.

"Please," she whispers. "Please, Dane."

"I love when you beg." I don't let up on the punishing thrusts or pulling her into them so I slide even deeper. "Let me feel how good you milk my cock, baby. Come for your husband," I rumble just as dominantly as I do possessively. I want her to know she's mine. Not in a crazy stalker way, but in that protective, comforting way. The knowledge that she's woven herself deep into my heart.

Her back arches. Her nails dig even more into me, and she scratches across my shoulder blades. Keeping her eyes open for me like the good girl she is, she releases. "Ah! Yes… Yes, Dane!"

I let out a roar as I come at the same time as her. "Skyla!" I pump jets of come into her as our hips jerk against each other. We both pant and moan.

Skyla's pussy squeezes my dick with each and every spasm as she orgasms. I can feel her juices and mine intermingling and dripping down my balls. Not willing to lose our connection so quickly, I stay seated deeply inside her. I rub her hips and sides. I kiss all over her face and neck as she moans and whimpers while she comes down. She runs her fingers lightly over my back again, but this time, she's feeling all of the scratches left. Her marks.

What feels like hours later, my dick slides out on its own. We both groan at the loss, but instead of reaching down and getting myself hard again so I can bury myself inside her, I decide to be a good boy and get up. I walk to the bathroom as Skyla watches me through hooded, satisfied eyes. I grab a washcloth and wet it down with warm water. I clean myself off, rinse out the cloth, hang it over an empty towel rack, then grab another one for Skyla. I wet that one down with hot water so by the time I get to her, it will be the perfect temp.

After cleaning my girl up and taking care of the cloth, I crawl back into bed. Skyla says no words. She curls herself into me and hums before she passes out. I barely have the blankets around us before she's adorably and softly snoring.

I pull her as close to me as possible. I shut out the lamp on the nightstand, and not long after, I myself am pulled into a deep and content sleep.

Chapter Fourteen

☙ Skyla ❧

I jerk awake at the sound of a blaring alarm that sounds similar to an air raid siren. I look around the room wildly as I bolt to a sitting position.

"Dane!" I shriek. I turn to where he was wrapped around me in the bed and find he isn't there. It's dark in the room, though, so I can't see if he's near.

"I'm right here, baby. Come with me." His hand is suddenly on my arm, and he's pulling me out of the bed. "Put these on. Hurry up."

My eyes are barely adjusted to the dark, but I don't question him. It feels like a t-shirt and sweats, but they're too big for me. They must belong to him. I can see the outline of him pulling something on. I assume he's also getting dressed, and he must see better than me because as soon as I get the sweats pulled up, he's pulling me towards the door.

"Dane, what's going on?" I instinctively try to cover my ears as soon as he opens the bedroom door. The alarm seems so much louder out here. In reality, it's probably because there are multiple alarms or something going off at the same time. There's a red light flashing, bathing the hallway in an eerie red glow.

"Lieutenant! What's happening?" Aimee screams from her bedroom door down the hall from us. Her ears are covered. She looks and sounds just as panicked as me.

"I'll explain later! Come here!" Dane gestures with his gun I just noticed he's carrying. Aimee wastes no time running down the hall towards us. "Grab Skyla's hand. Do not let go of her under any circumstances. Skyla, same for you. Don't let go of me or her. Understand?"

I nod, terrified out of my mind. "Yes, sir!" I manage to squeak out. I'm trembling. So is Aimee. Dane is rock solid and steady. He'll never understand how grateful I am for that.

Holding my hand, Dane leads with his gun. Aimee and I follow his command to not let go of each other. I hold his hand just as tightly as she's holding mine. We're moving quickly, and once we reach the stairs, we're running.

I glance around the second we reach the bottom of the stairs and notice that all of the windows have a steel plate in front of them. Dane leads us down the hall towards his office, but just before he reaches it, he stops. He pulls me closer to him before pushing me against the wall. He lets go of my hand and pushes Aimee against the wall next to me.

"Back flat. Stay against the wall. Don't let go of each other. Don't move." Dane is in full Lieutenant mode. The commands are given with a dark edge to his voice I know he reserves for when he's on missions and giving orders. There's a dominance to it, but it's different from what he uses on me.

All Aimee and I can do is nod wide eyed as our eyes bounce from him to everywhere else like the house is about to become a house of horrors. Like everything around us is about to become live beings and try to kill us. Drag us into the depths of the house.

Dane presses a code into something that looks a little bit like a flat tablet inside the wall. He waits a few seconds, completely still. The door next to us and in front of him suddenly starts to slide open. I watch it, fascinated, but I don't have much time because Dane is pushing both me and Aimee through it as quickly as it opens. He presses a button, and I watch it close. He enters a code into another pad.

"Welcome, Mr. Michaels. Please enter your security code," a female voice says. It sounds anything but robotic, and I'm completely impressed. Dane enters a few numbers again. "Thank you, Mr. Michaels. Access granted. Full lockdown initiated."

Dane pulls us through another door into a corridor that is better lit than his house. "Down here is a shelter. We just had it built. We've done drills. We know it works. We use it when our property has been infiltrated or if we get information that we're going to end up in an air raid."

"An... air raid? Like bombs?" I nearly scream, my panic reaching new levels. He practically drags me and Aimee down the steep stairs, but even in the chaos, I can't help but notice the incredible care he portrays to make sure we don't trip on the metal stairs. Especially since we're all barefoot and the stairs don't feel that great on our feet.

"Yes, baby. Like bombs."

"So, it's a bomb shelter," Aimee says more matter-of-factly than I can even process.

"Oh my God... Dane, I... knew this was happening and being built, but I thought it was just a place to hide if... things..." I don't even know what to say. I hear a loud bang above us. It sounds more like an explosion than it should, and I scream as I trip.

Dane manages to steady me before I take both him and Aimee down with me. "Baby, I promise. I'll explain everything more clearly, but we need to get to safety."

"How are you so calm?" I yell as uncontrollable tears start springing from my eyes. "What's happening?"

He doesn't answer me, but he doesn't have to. I know we're under attack. Everyone's worst nightmare has come true, and it's all because of me. I did this. I brought this to their feet. It's my fault Aimee was pulled into his web of lies and violent deceit. This, all of it, is all on me.

As I uncontrollably sob, Dane pulls us down another hallway in this underground maze. He stops in front of another pad and enters a code. This time, though, I'm taken aback as Nick Crane's face appears.

"Code," he growls as a pad of numbers appears. Dane enters it with steady hands, his gun still firmly in his grip. Nick's face comes back. "Who's with you?"

"Skyla and Aimee." He moves just enough so Nick can see the two of us huddled behind Dane.

"Anyone else in the hall with you?"

Dane looks down the hall. "No. But there's footsteps. Don't know who it is yet."

"Wait." Nick's face disappears, and I squeak.

"What? Tell him to let us in!" Aimee screeches, now in just as much of a panic as me. Her eyes dart everywhere.

"Quiet," Dane commands. We both shut our mouths and huddle as close to each other as we can.

The footsteps get louder.

Closer.

I fight with all I am to not scream and run the opposite way, but I wouldn't know which way to run anyway. The footsteps sound like they're surrounding us. My heart is going to beat out of my chest and probably explode when it hits the cement floor underneath me.

"It's Josh," Dane rumbles.

My eyes fly open. I let out a relieved breath, but the adrenaline running through still makes me want to flee. I'm sure if I let go of Dane or Aimee, I'll shoot through the roof. I don't care that it is cement. Or a billion feet of metal.

Josh quickly enters a code, and Nick's face appears again. "Code." Nick says as the keypad appears once more. Josh says nothing as he enters a code. I don't understand why it's entered twice, but I don't care. I just want out of this hallway. Nick's face appears again. "Who's with you?"

"Arianna and Dallas."

"Anyone else in the hall?"

"Dane, Skyla, and Aimee," Josh says.

The wall in front of us begins to slide open, and I stumble back in surprise. I don't know what I expected, but I didn't see anything indicating this was an entrance to anything. For some reason, I thought the floor would open up and we'd slide down through a couple of levels of darkness on a giant slide as we screamed and land on a fluffy air pillow or something.

Dane pulls Aimee and I ahead of him, and walks in behind us. Josh does exactly the same thing with Arianna and Dallas. I blink in shock as the wall behind us closes. In front of me is nothing short of a giant living room complete with an eighty inch TV mounted to the wall. There's enough room to fit at least thirty people in here comfortably while giving everyone a place to sit, but I notice the room expands to an even further depth than I'd first seen, making it even larger.

There's comfortable furniture. The cement is carpeted and soft. It feels warm on my freezing feet that I'm sure is caked with dirt. I don't want to move because I don't want the pretty carpet to be tarnished.

"You can come in, you know," Jessa Crane says quietly as she rocks her son, Jackson. Jason is washing her bare feet. I just look up at Dane for direction.

"Go have a seat," Dane whispers. He kisses my head.

"What about you?" I whisper back.

"Let me take care of you. Go sit down, baby."

I nod and do as he says. I sit next to Jessa, suddenly more exhausted than I can explain. As soon as my butt hits the cushions of the couch, I'm wanting to just melt into it. Aimee settles next to me and must feel the same way because she lets out a small whimper.

Nick stands in the middle of the room with his tablet asking each person who dares to enter the same questions he did us. I close my eyes slowly and let out a calming breath while I release the death grip I have on Aimee's hand, but I jerk slightly as my eyes fly open when I feel a warm cloth on my feet.

I look down at Dane and nearly melt into goop when I see he's washing my feet. It's such a simple action, but the love behind it is so enduring and beautiful.

What's even more beautiful is he does the same for Aimee, who whimpers in relief. I don't blame her. It felt nice to get the dirt and grime off them. When he finishes, he hands us each a pair of warm socks.

It seems like hours, but it's only been minutes when the last person arrives. Ryan Crane enters by himself, no doubt only after ensuring everyone else got to safety. I don't know all of the protocols. I don't know why Josh arrived with Arianna and not her son. All I know is each move is meticulous and very much planned. I'd never question that.

What I do question, however, is why Dane looks like he's going into battle. He's strapping on a bulletproof vest and talking to Ryan.

"Josh, please. Please don't," Dallas sniffles. Her arms are locked around Josh's waist as he hugs her. They're close to me, and I can't help but turn to them. Not that I mean to eavesdrop. I'm just still not fully certain I'm not dreaming.

"You know I have to. It's my job to keep you and this family safe."

"I know, but I'm so scared." She grips him even tighter.

"You're safe. You're gonna stay that way."

She looks up at him, tears streaming down her cheeks. "What about you? You can't protect anyone if -"

"Dallas," Josh rumbles low and deeply. She closes her mouth instantly. "I promise I'm going to do all I can to come back. But this is my job. My job is to keep you safe; this family safe. I need you to be strong for me and trust me."

She nods but buries her face in his chest once more. I look up at Dane once more as my face falls. I stand and walk to him, hugging myself. When I reach him, Ryan smiles softly and steps away to speak with Nick. Nick's wife, Dani, is curled up on the couch with her knees to her chest.

"What's going on?" I ask softly.

"Nick is going to explain everything to everyone," Dane says, his voice low. He slings a long range rifle over his back. "To make it short, though. Zeke, our head of security, saw something a little odd on the cameras earlier. He'd been doing some research as some guards went to check out what he saw. While he was researching, he caught wind of a threat directed at Josh."

"What kind of a threat?" I ask, truly not wanting to know the answer.

"A bomb threat. An attack from the air. Turns out what Zeke saw were targets that were dropped in. He thinks they missed their mark because they're in the oddest of places, and I agree. I don't think the plan was well thought out. As soon as he found all of that, though, he alerted both Josh and Ryan. They both called contacts. They thought everything was okay. They got their contacts to declare this area a no fly zone. Air Traffic Control at Chicago's airport has been diverting planes around us. It's all been good."

"So..., why the air raid siren? Why are we down here?"

"Because someone ignored the no fly zone warning. Zeke got a call from a contact saying there was an unauthorized flying object in the zone. He immediately activated our emergency system. You'll notice Robby isn't down here, and neither is Lance. That's because they're on top of the guard's quarters. They both shot down a couple of drones, but one of them was missed. Zeke said that it crashed near the water and took out some of the wall. He thinks it was intentional to breach our security. Whoever did it, didn't count on us having multiple levels of security."

"So, where are you going?" I nearly whisper.

Dane finally pulls me in his arms. Just as Dallas was with Josh, I burrow into his chest and hug him as hard as I can. "I have to -"

I shake my head and hug him harder. "Don't tell me. I'm sorry I asked. I don't want to know. I just want you back safe... and whole."

He runs his fingers through my hair and tugs just enough to make me look at him. I love when he does that. I don't know why, but I really, really love it. When my eyes meet his, it's all I can do to stay on my feet because his eyes are burning with a level of passion I've never experienced. Love. Unbridled love.

"I'm searching the perimeter. Making sure it's safe. You'll have some guards here. Cole will be here. Jason, Chase, Nick, and Alex will all be here." He leans in and kisses me.

"I need you to come back."

He cups my cheeks and kisses me deeply and sweetly. He pulls back slowly, leaving me breathless and yearning for more. "I'm coming back."

I don't know if he's just saying those words to appease me, or if he really means them, but I take them at face value and let them seep into my heart.

I hold onto him as long as I can as Ryan and the others kiss and hug their loved ones. I'm amazed at how the other women are taking it. It's like it's another day for them. It's me and Dallas who seem to be taking it the hardest.

In fact, when they leave to take care of what they need to, it's me and Dallas who are huddled together in an oversized chair. Aimee is burrowed between Aiden and Lucas. Dani is snuggled with Nick. Arianna is making drinks for everyone with all of the kids at her side helping her. It would be adorable if I wasn't so terrified.

As the hours roll on, the mood begins to lighten just a little. We all walk around the massive underground bunker and are amazed. It's just like a giant mansion. If I ignore the fact that there are no windows and the entire thing is reinforced in feet upon feet of steel and who knows what else, I could make myself believe this is just a huge, shared mansion. All of the rooms, the bathrooms, the kitchen, the living area, and the pantry are truly incredible.

There's enough food in here to last a long time. There's electricity. Running water. I won't pretend to understand for a second how it all works or how we're able to get fresh air in here and not suffocate, but I'm grateful for it. We could all probably live here comfortably for years. It feels just like home.

Only it isn't home. Dane is home. The bunker offers everything except the one thing I both want and need.

Dane.

Chapter Fifteen

☙ Dane ☙

(One Week Later)

"Hold up. You want to what?" I ask Aiden.

"I want to go back in. They didn't find anything with the warrant, but they found other stuff that could lead to the other shit we're looking for. I also think New York needs to raid his office and penthouse. And I want to go into the one he has here."

I lean back in my chair pushing the top of my pen so it clicks. God only knows why, but it's a comfort to me. "Show me."

Aiden sits down in front of my desk with a grin and starts pointing shit out in the reports from some people I assigned to carry out a search while my team was in the hospital and recovering. The search was carried out with Lucinio Mafia guards guarding the perimeter of the house.

"Like this. They let this go, but this could've connected to the bomb." He points to copper wire found in a kitchen drawer but not recovered. Just mentioned in the report.

"Wiring and casing was in the warrant on things to search for. Why didn't they take that?"

"I don't know. But there's more." He points to something else. "Residue. Not collected or brought to the lab for testing. And then there's blood. Not collected. His bedroom was never searched. Several rooms were never searched."

I don't move from my position. I keep clicking the pen as I think. "I'll get Josh to help expedite the warrant I request here and get someone with NYPD to request one he can get expedited. Gather a team, but do it quietly. We're down Aimee. Don't ask any of the people involved in the last one. These reports belong to three people that I never appointed to do the search. It means we have a leak among them."

"Maybe we should work with Taylor and his team on this one. I feel like it's sensitive and needs immediate attention."

I nod as I lean forward. "I'll talk to him. Go tell Cole the plan. Be discreet."

"You got it boss."

I wait for him to leave and close my door behind him before I call Taylor. Aiden is absolutely correct. We need to keep this within our circle this time. Obviously, I can't trust anyone in this fucking department. Maybe we need Ryan and Josh to do another clean up. Take out the fuckers who obviously value that extra incentive to cover evidence.

"What's up, Dane?"

"I wish I could say nothing. Take me off speaker."

I hear some rustling. "Off speaker. What's going on, man?"

"I just saw the reports from the search on Thurston's house. Fuck, things were left that should have been taken. Rooms weren't searched. Nothing was found in that house. There should've been. Copper wire found in a kitchen drawer. Not collected. Blood. A residue. Not collected and tested. Powder in the bathroom. Not collected or tested. Basement. Not searched. There was a shed that they searched on the property and found nothing."

Taylor is quiet for a few moments before he sighs. "You think he paid some people off."

"No doubt in my mind. That can be taken care of later, though. I'm drafting a warrant request as we speak for his residence and his penthouse. I think we need to get Josh involved and have Lance check for any other residences or storage units. He has to be hiding shit somewhere. I mean, we're lucky we got all of those targets removed. We're lucky those drones were shot down. But we were most lucky that we were able to recover them and recover the bombs attached to them. There has to be somewhere he's storing this shit."

Taylor chuckles. "I'm still pissed that one exploded above my sidewalk. Nikki doesn't like that the kids can see it and be reminded of that night. I think if I let her loose, she'd kill everyone involved with this herself."

It's my turn to chuckle. "That girl can be frightening when she wants to be."

"The quiet ones always are."

I can't help but think of Skyla. She's probably the quietest of them all, but I'd bet everything I own that she's a supernova underneath it all. "I think he's hiding the makings of them somewhere. He has to be," I repeat. "My bet is he has a storage unit somewhere or he flies them in from New York."

"I'd say it's both. He probably flies shit in from New York and hides it somewhere here."

"Could be. Which is why I was thinking of calling Josh in. Getting him to call his contacts in New York."

"I think that's a good idea. Situations like this are perks of being in the family."

"You're not kidding. I was also thinking when we do the raids, we need to do them simultaneously. Me one place. You another. Cole another, if we find storage lockers. And then Nick somewhere else. And we just take people from our teams."

"Oof… That's stretching us pretty thin. I'd say ask for mafia protection and assistance on the entrance. We can handle the search, but we need more than a couple of people to enter and make sure we're good."

"Yeah, you're right. I thought of that, then talked myself out of it." I'm always grateful I have Taylor to talk through things with me. He may be younger than me, but I'm still pretty new to the leading my own team thing. For many years, Taylor was my leader. In many ways, he still is.

"Get Josh on a threeway."

I didn't know how much I needed it, but I'm grateful for the leadership because I feel like I'm messing up left and right since the day Aimee, Aiden, and Lucas got hurt. I'm pretty good about shaking myself out of thoughts like that. I get them from time to time, but this time has been more difficult.

"What's up, big bro?" Josh teases when he answers. Who knew I needed that, too?

I grin. "I have you on a threeway with Taylor."

"Uh oh," Josh rumbles. "Sounds serious. What do you need?" His tone of voice has gone from friendly and brotherly to very much business.

"Well, a few things. I hate to bring it to you."

"It's my job, Dane. Tell me."

"I need a warrant expedited for Thurston's residences. All of them. Here and in New York," I blurt out.

"We also need Lance to do his thing and tell us if there are any storage units here or in New York. Tell us if he has any other places he owns," Taylor says. "We want to raid his headquarters in New York. Anywhere he is, we want to raid it."

I can hear Josh's hand running down his face. I sigh. "I know this is a big ask."

"What are you hoping to get out of this?" Josh asks.

"Glad you asked," Taylor says. "The truth."

"I have reports from the raid we did on the mansion. There's a lot of fucked up bullshit here. There's stuff listed in this report that was never gathered. Blood samples. Residue samples. A fucking copper wire. They had full reign of the house. Rooms weren't looked at. The basement and shed weren't searched."

Josh is silent for several moments. "I'll pull contacts. First, I need Robby in on this helping Lance. There's a lot of ground to cover in a short amount of time. Robby can help. As for the other locations, you're going to want to do this simultaneously. What if we got the FBI and Interpol involved? I can pull them. Make it more... legal, I guess. Not have me and the mafia raiding with you."

"No way can police departments handle something this large scale," Taylor says. He doesn't say it, but I know he agrees with Josh.

Typically, cops don't like federal agencies getting involved. They create a lot of problems for us. Once they're involved, it's their case. They don't play nice with jurisdiction because they believe the whole of the United States and several international countries becomes their playing field. Truthfully, they're right, but cops don't like losing cases. Especially like this one that could make or break an entire career.

Luckily for me, Josh's contacts aren't like that. They'll come in, help out, and leave. The case still belongs to us because they know Josh will more than likely throw something larger at them. Something they'll get exclusive access to and credit for, even though it's just them helping out Josh and being his cover.

"The answer is a no brainer, really. You know I'm fine with it. I'll take all the help we can get. At least I know we'll be able to trust the people we're working with." I lean back in my chair with my eyes on the door. I sigh. "I just want this shit over with. For Skyla's sake."

"I know, man," Josh says. "We'll deal with it as swiftly as possible."

"We still have that arrest warrant, too," Taylor says. "No one has been able to find him. He hasn't gone into the office in New York, and he fled the mansion. They checked the penthouse and staked it out. He hasn't been there either."

"Then we need to start upping surveillance," Josh says like it's an answer we should've come up with on our own. He's right, honestly. "We've been looking for him, but time to double up on surveillance. Simple as that. If our contacts can't find him, Chicago's Golden Boys can't, then time for us to step even harder. Let them know we're here."

"Why does that sound more scary than Ryan?" Taylor asks. I can see the signature cocky grin he always wears even though he's not in the same room. It's burned in my brain. "Fucking shivers."

Josh laughs. "Come on, Lieutenant. Let the big dog out of his cage."

"Fuck." I crack up. "Like you need permission to be let loose."

"Just being respectful of my local law enforcement," Josh drawls. We all laugh, and it eases the tension tremendously. "Alright. Let me get them on storage units. They have all residences, but they'll double check. We're watching everything, too. We haven't seen hide nor hair of him either."

"Then it ain't just us. Good to know," I say. "I'll work on the warrant."

"Don't turn it in until we find everything we need to know. I'll get my contacts together. As usual, we do it all my way. You two get the credit."

"Goes without saying," Taylor says. "I don't know why you and Ryan seem to have a need to reiterate that."

Josh chuckles low. "Because we know you and Dane are loose fucking cannons."

"Asshole," I say with a laugh. He might be right about that, too, though. I think if he or Ryan gave Taylor and I free reign, they'd have their work cut out for them in keeping our asses out of prison. Not a place for a cop to be. There's special treatment for cops who end up on the other side of those walls. I don't want any part of that shit.

After we hang up, I get to work on the warrants and let Taylor fill in both of our teams on the new plan. I make sure I call Skyla to check in. I know Josh well. We won't be hitting anywhere tonight unless there's no choice. So, I don't cancel dinner with her.

Spending time with her is my favorite time of the day. We've spent the last week being with each other as much as possible. I'd say it's the honeymoon phase, but really it's no different than how it was before.

Except the sex. Which is fucking incredible and only gets better and better.

The rest of the afternoon goes quickly. When it's time to head out, I lock my paperwork for the warrant in a locked drawer in my desk. I'm shutting everything down just as my cellphone starts ringing. I pick up immediately when I see Damon's name.

"Hey, Damon. Wh-"

"Accident," he grunts out. "We're fine. Josh is coming. Squad was involved."

I furrow my brows. "Um... Say that again?" No way I heard that right.

"Sideswiped us." He groans. "Fuck, my fucking ankle."

I quickly turn to my laptop, the one thing I haven't shut down yet. "What's the number? Can you see?"

"Uh... Nine-nine-two-one. That's the number on the side."

I quickly enter the number and look up the squad to see who was assigned to it today. I'm not at all surprised when I see it's one of the fuckers who was on the search and gave a report that was all sorts of fucked up.

"Get off the fucking phone!" someone yells on the other end of the line. I assume at Damon.

"Don't hang up the phone. I'm grabbing Cole right now. Cole!" I bark loud enough for anyone on the other side of my door in the bullpen to hear.

"I said get off the phone!"

"I have your Lieutenant on the phone, asshole," Damon growls dangerously.

"He's one of the guys who was on the search at the mansion. Gave me a fucked up report. A lot of shit was hidden."

While I shut my laptop down, I drop my phone in my haste to get to Damon. The second I'm bending down to get it, Cole opens the door to my office.

"What's up, Lieuten-"

He's cut off by the sound of glass shattering. I look over my shoulder and see the bulletproof glass of my office window has been broken.

I don't have time to figure out how because I hear what sounds suspiciously like a gunshot echoing through the air. Pain shoots through my entire body, but I can't tell where it's radiating from. I drop to the ground.

Around me I hear a lot of screaming.

More shooting.

Swearing.

I try to fight it, but the blackness surrounding me soon envelops me and drags me with it into the dark shadows of hell.

Chapter Sixteen

❦ skyla ❦

I'm panicking.

I can't breathe.

I'm on my knees in the middle of the hospital waiting room, and I'm about to die.

I know nothing. All I know is my husband was shot.

In his office.

At fucking work!

Don't they have bulletproof glass at headquarters? Shouldn't they have that for every police station in the world? They'd want to protect their officers, right? That's a thing that happens, right?

"Breathe…," Austin rumbles next to me. His arms wrap around me. As per usual, I start to calm, but it doesn't last long.

"I need to know if he's okay." I hiccup and hug myself even tighter than I already was as I tremble. I don't bother wiping away my tears. Let them fall. If he's -

No.

Absolutely not.

I will not allow myself to think that way. He'll be fine. He has to be. I won't survive if he isn't. I just found the strength to open myself fully to him and completely accept his love. I'm not letting it end like this. It won't. It would destroy me if it did.

Before I start sobbing again, the door to the private waiting area opens. I scramble up when I see Josh coming in. He's looking down at his phone, but I don't care what he's doing.

I launch at him, nearly choking on my tears. "Tell me how he is! Please! Please tell me he's okay." I look up at him, the sobs overtaking me again as I grip his shirt.

Josh wraps his arms around me and looks over his shoulder. "Dr. Freeman is on the way in. He was behind me, but he must've gotten stopped."

"Please just tell me!" Josh's blue, silk dress shirt is going to have a dark stain from my tears, but I know he won't care. So, I just grip him harder and let him hold me up because I'm about to collapse again.

"Ssh...," he rumbles soothingly as he hugs me. "Dr. Freeman can explain everything better than me. I can tell you how it happened, but I can't tell anything more than -" Josh cuts off when the door opens once more.

"Doc? What's going on? Is he gonna make it?" Cole asks. He's not really in much better shape than me. He's distraught. His eyes are red from his own tears. I didn't realize just how close Cole and Dane were until today.

I feel someone standing next to us. I look up to see Taylor. He's another person I hadn't really realized Dane was so close to. Truthfully, Dane is like family to everyone here, and there are a lot of people here. Everyone from both the Crane and Lucino clans are in this room. They've all come together, and it's a heartwarming sight to behold. I've never been so grateful for all of them as I am now.

"He's okay. He's gonna make it," Dr. Freeman says, squeezing my arm. If Josh wasn't hugging me so tightly, I'd be on the ground. "The bullet went through. That was a stroke of luck. It nicked his collarbone, but for the most part, there's no damage. It was lucky he'd bent down to pick up his phone."

"So, he's gonna be okay? Can I see him?" I ask hopefully.

"You can as soon as we get him into a room. He's in recovery right now." Dr. Freeman puts his hand on my shoulder and gives it a gentle squeeze. "He's going to make a full recovery. In a few weeks, he'll be saving the world again."

I sniffle but nod, feeling completely selfish that I don't want him to go back to work. I want to just keep him at home where he'll be safe.

But then a horrible thought occurs.

I look up at Josh. "How? How did this happen? Are the windows not bulletproof? How did he get shot in his office in a building that's supposed to be one of the safest buildings in the city?"

"Good question. Complicated answer." Josh steers me towards Austin and Rachael, Austin's girlfriend. He settles me between them and stands to address everyone. "Firstly, Dane is going to be okay. Dr. Freeman just explained that he's in recovery and doing well. The bullet nicked his collarbone, but went through. He'll be good as new in a few weeks." He waits as everyone sighs in relief. "As for what happened, a military grade explosive round was used to first shatter the glass. We found the spent casing. We think there were two gunmen. One to shoot out the glass. The other one shot Dane. The shot was too quick for it to be lined up by the same person."

"We recovered the bullets," Taylor chips in.

My eyes widen. "Oh my God. Did you say military grade...?"

Josh quirks an eyebrow. "Yes."

"Thurston had some kind of partnership with certain branches of the military. Special branches. Like special ops or something. I was never privy to that. He handled all of that on his own. I never saw anything in the company financials about it. I always thought he was padding his own account, but I could never prove anything." I put my hands over my face and drop my elbows on my knees as I groan. "This is my fault."

"Skyla. No. It's not your fault," Josh says. "Lance, I need you on that. Find whatever you can."

"Robby will handle the other part dealing with storage units and stuff," Lance says. "I'll take this."

As the conversation goes on around me, I sink further and further into the abyss. No matter what he says, this is my fault. I should've figured out a way to stop all of this a long time ago. I should've stuck with him and tried to find all of the dirty secrets I knew he was hiding. And if I died in the process, at least I tried and died trying to save people that Thurston obviously intends to hurt.

I feel like hours go by, and I come to one single conclusion. Thurston isn't going to stop. Not unless I walk back into his stronghold. He's going to keep going after all of my loved ones until I have nothing left.

I need to be strong this time.

I need to be the one to protect them.

I can't be weak Skyla anymore. I have to stand on my own two feet and be brave against him. It's the only way to keep everyone else safe. Otherwise, he'll systematically destroy my entire carefully built world and everyone in it.

By the time Dr. Freeman comes to get me to see Dane, I've made my decision. It's a hard one. One I know I won't survive, but it's what needs to be done to save the man I love and this family that has become my own.

When I sit down in the chair Dr. Freeman put next to the bed, I'm grateful to see Dane is still sleeping. He looks so peaceful. Angelic even. His beautiful personality underneath his gruff exterior is shining through right now, proving to me once more that while what I'm about to do is difficult, it's the best decision.

I breathe in deeply and take his hand. I want to close my eyes, but I don't. I need to make sure I memorize every feature of his face, his body, everything about him. That's what I'll take with me when I walk out that door.

I lean my cheek against his hand. "I love you. I love you so much, and I want you to always know that. I want those words to permeate your body, mind, heart, and soul so you never ever doubt why I'm doing what I'm doing." I swallow the lump in my throat and blink back my tears. "You're the most wonderful person I've ever had the pleasure of knowing. You showed me that I'm not the damaged goods I thought I was. You made me truly see myself through your eyes. I understand now. I understand the selflessness that you showed me all of the time; the sacrifice you made for me every single day. And now it's my turn to show you that unconditional love I feel but never knew how to express." Silent tears begin to fall, but I keep going. "This is not goodbye. No matter what happens to me, I'll always be with you. I'll be in your heart and rooting for your happiness, even though it can't be with me at your side."

I can't resist the need I have to hold him; to feel his warm body against mine one last time. Being careful of his bandaging, I shift and wrap my arms around him. I lay my head on his chest and hug him as hard as I dare while I cry. The tears are never going to stop, so after a few moments, I force myself to pull back.

The last thing I do is take off my ring. I take his hand and push it as far down on his pinkie as I can. To keep the light from hitting the diamond and instantly alerting anyone to the ring before he notices it, I turn it so the diamond is underneath.

Wiping my eyes the best I can and hoping they stay dry for long enough to make my escape, I lean down and kiss him.

"I love you. So, so much, Dane. Thank you. Thank you so much for showing me what true love really is and that I'm worthy of it and deserve it. I'll never forget that, and I'll always carry my love for you and yours for me with me until my last breath."

Before I start crying again, I kiss him once more and hurry out of the room. I check up and down the hallway before darting in the opposite direction of the private waiting area. I don't want to chance anyone seeing me.

I find a stairwell and duck into it. I run down a few flights before I dare take a breath. I feel like a teenager sneaking out, but it's how it has to be. I listen and look for any movement. When I notice none, I start walking down the stairs at a far less suspicious pace and take out my phone. I take a breath and dial the one number I never wanted to dial ever again.

"T-Rac Merc," a sweet voice answers. "How may I direct your call?"

"I'd like to speak with Thurston Maxwell, please. Tell him it's Skyla Michaels." I deliberately use my married name. It's my own way of sending a message. He might be about to get what he wants, but I'm not bowing down.

"I'm sorry. Mr. Maxwell isn't accepting calls right -"

"Then tell him Skyla Winters wants to speak with him. Immediately," I say through gritted teeth and a little dangerously.

It must work, though, because seconds later, there's elevator music playing in my ear. I continue down the stairs as I wait for my nightmare to answer. He'll answer if I use that name. I should've thought of that. He'd have them all on alert. He'd force me to use that name if I wanted to reach him.

Just when I reach the bottom floor, he finally does. "Skyla," he breathes deeply through the phone. I used to love that. Now, it just makes me sick to my stomach.

"Assure me that you won't touch them. Any of them. My brother. Rachael. Dane. The Crane's. The Lucinio's. The kids. None of them."

He chuckles low. "Well, that doesn't seem like a fair deal. What do I get, baby?"

Him calling me that name makes my skin crawl. "Me," I say simply, even though it makes me want to throw up.

He's silent for a long while. "Where are you?"

"Assure me first. Or you'll never get to me." I know those words are true. He'd never get to me, but he'd do all he can to destroy everyone around me.

"Fine. Assured. Now, where are you?"

It may seem strange, but the one good thing about Thurston is he's never gone back on his word. He never promised me he wouldn't hit me again, but he did promise that no one would know about it. He was right. No one did. He also assured me that as long as I played ball, he'd leave my brother alone. It was also something he never took back. He's never gone after Austin, even after we fled, it was always me he targeted.

"Northwestern Memorial. East side in the stairwell."

"I'll meet you in the parking lot. Anyone follows you, I go back on my promise and kill them all. Got me?"

I panic. "I can't guarantee that, Thurston. You know Josh has people everywhere. I promise if anyone comes out, I don't know about it. I'm not trying anything. I just want them safe."

He growls a little, but it comes out more like a rumble. It's something that used to make me wet, but not anymore. Now, if it's not Dane, it makes me want to jump off a building.

I briefly contemplate that. Would it be a better choice than the one I'm making? Surely putting myself back into the grasp of a psychopath is a far worse decision.

"Don't hang up this phone, Skyla. I'll be there. The second you disconnect, though, they're all fucked."

I take a breath and nod. "I won't hang up."

"Good girl. I'll give you a nice reward for that. The more good you do, the less severe your punishment for fucking running will be."

I swallow. Hard. The fear he instills is unlike anything I could ever describe, but it's not as strong as the love I have for Dane; for my family, found and otherwise.

"I'll obey, Thurston. I promise."

"I trust you. I don't trust them. There's a man on a motorcycle pulling into the parking lot now. Walk out the side door."

Quick.

Too quick. It's like he was watching and knew where I was this whole time.

"Yes, sir," I say the moment I see the motorcycle. I swallow the bile calling him 'sir' creates. I like calling Dane that. I love it. I don't like saying it to Thurston. It doesn't feel right. It never has.

"Get on the back of the bike. You're a human shield for him. He'll take you to me. Don't fuck up."

I jump when the door to the stairwell opens and almost die in fear when I see Racheal. "Oh my God," I whisper.

"Skyla? Are you okay?" Racheal asks. "What are you doing in here?"

"Ignore her. Get on the bike, Skyla. Toss your phone as soon as you're on it."

I do exactly as I'm told because I don't want her getting hurt for following me. I turn and run out of the side door. I jump on the back of the bike and toss my phone without hanging up. I wrap around whoever this biker is and squeeze my eyes shut. I press myself against him and act like a human shield.

"Hold on. Stick close," he rumbles. He takes off so fast that I nearly fall off the bike. I hold onto him even tighter.

"Skyla!" I hear Racheal scream behind me.

As much as I want to, I don't look back...

Chapter Seventeen

☙ Dane ☙

(Two Months Later)

I let out a roar of frustration and slam my fists against the cement wall of the abandoned warehouse.

Two months.

It's been two months since I last saw my girl.

Two months since I woke up from a goddamn near death experience only to find out Skyla was gone. No one knew what the fuck happened, but I do. I know it deep within my soul because I know her and her heart.

She saw me in that hospital bed and couldn't think of anything else but protecting me the only way she could.

Giving herself to Thurston fucking Maxwell. Calling him and letting herself be pulled back under his power and control. All because she wants to protect me.

I'm never going to forget that day. When I woke up, my first thought was Skyla. I could see her as I was opening my eyes, but I couldn't make sense of the damn words flowing from her mouth. Something about how she loves me. How she'll carry it with her until her last breath. Then she faded, but it scared me enough that I fought through the remaining haze. I tried to chase her, but I couldn't move. It took my body a few minutes to fully come to.

By the time I could gather myself enough to push the fucking button for help, she was long gone. When Dr. Freeman saw Skyla wasn't in the room with me like she was supposed to be, according to him, he called for Josh instantly. Just as Josh was walking in, he got a call from Racheal. She was screaming and crying. He couldn't get anything out of her except that she was in the parking lot. He sent guards for her.

As soon as she got up to my room, she was in hysterics, screaming how Skyla was gone. How she fled and got on the back of a motorcycle. She saw the back of the jacket of the biker. It was clearly Ruthless Warriors. The person, who she identified as definitely male, was wearing a helmet. She said Skyla looked terrified as she wrapped around him like she was shielding him from something.

And she said she threw her damn cellphone.

"We're gonna find her. You know that," Cole says, squeezing my shoulder.

If I could grip the wall, I'd shatter it. Instead, though, I hit it, open palm, a few more times just to get some of my aggravation out. "How the fuck are we always so close but miss her?" I seethe through gritted teeth.

"There has to be some way that he's getting information," Taylor tells me as he leans against the wall next to me.

I press my head against the cold, cracked cement and close my eyes. "It's been too long. What -"

"No," Cole cuts me off. "We're not thinking like that. We know she's alive."

"How? How do we know? I've seen no evidence saying she's alive or dead," I growl.

"Simple." Taylor pats me on the back. "You're still standing. We all believe we'd feel it if our significant others were in danger or hurt or, God forbid, dead. We definitely believe you'd feel it, too."

I open my eyes and turn with a sigh. I lean my back against the wall next to Taylor and shake my head. "If I see one fucking mark on her when we find her, so help Josh. He won't be able to stop me from taking the fucking shot."

"I'm not sure he'd even try. He'd just make you wait until he got the information out of him that he'd want. Then he'd probably just walk away and leave him in your capable hands." Taylor chuckles. "Or maybe he'd follow a little more in Ryan's footsteps and make sure your hands aren't bloodied."

I know the answer. I know he won't let me near Thurston's demise, but man. Fucking envisioning every possible way I could kill him with my bare hands is the only thing getting me through this. Well, that and my love for Skyla; her last words to me; the way she confessed her love by doing what she's doing to protect me and this family.

"We have to figure out how the fuck they know we're coming for them," I profess as I push off the wall. "They have to know something we don't, or we have a fucking mole." I hook my fingers in the straps of my bulletproof vest. "Where's Josh?"

"Floor below you," Josh's voice rumbles in the earpiece I forgot I'm wearing. "And Taylor's partially right. You're not getting near him for the kill, but I'll let you slap him around a little bit."

I chuckle at the tease in his voice. "Can't say I'd argue with that."

"You can try if you'd like. Won't get nowhere. Get down here. We're clearing out. There's nothing here," Josh commands.

"I don't know about nothing," Damon says. "We have those images Dane took of what could be a message."

I sigh as I lead Cole and Taylor out of the room we're in. We know it was the room they kept Skyla in because we found one of her shoes. I know it's hers because I bought it. It's a tan colored flat. A slip on that can be worn with anything. She loves them for that reason alone, but loves them even more because of the hidden message inside the shoe. We wrote it together.

I love you.

Simple words, but it made her feel close to me always. Strangely enough, I felt the same way. Knowing those words were close to her made me feel like my love was somehow enveloping her. When I realized she had these shoes on, her having them made me feel like I was protecting her somehow.

Now, one of those shoes is in my back pocket. The very one we wrote in. Seeing it shattered me even more than I already am, but the condition it's in is what broke me. It's tattered. Worn and torn. Dirty. I'm trying to keep myself from seeing her like the fucking shoe. Picturing her as my tough CFO who has the power to put anyone in their place with a look is keeping me going.

I feel completely crazy.

Once we reach the bottom of the stairs, I hand Josh my phone. He takes it with a raised eyebrow. "I can't," I say with a shrug. "I'm barely hanging on right now. I'm doing all I can to hold myself together. Sending that shit to Lance isn't in my realm of strength right now. All I want is my girl back. Two months, Josh."

"I know," Josh rumbles. "I know. I don't know how you're still functioning right now. If this happened to Dal-" He cuts himself as he looks down at my phone. He starts sending the images to Lance, but we all know what he was about to say. It's more obvious every day how in love with her he's fallen. The war he's waged with himself is similar to Ryan and Arianna. We've all seen it. "Everyone move out. Nothing more for us here." His voice is gruff. Everyone follows his direction. No one wants to be on his bad side.

"He's going to destroy himself if he doesn't just admit his feelings," Gavin says as he slides in the driver's seat of the SUV I just settled into the passenger seat of.

"You're not kidding," I say as Taylor and Cole settle in the backseat.

"What's the deal with him lately?" Cole asks. "Does he really not see that we all see what's going on?"

Gavin shrugs. "Josh has been through a lot of shit. He never thought he was worthy of Lyric, and he thinks it destroyed their relationship. He doesn't think he's worthy of anyone and is better off alone. He thinks he hurt Lyric when they broke up, but Lyric flat out told me it was never like that. She wasn't hurting. She started feeling like they were better off as best friends, but it had nothing to do with his image of himself. They just drifted apart. Josh blamed himself. Dallas is a lot younger than him."

I raise an eyebrow. "There's a huge age difference between you and Harleigh. Hell, even Alex and Raleigh. And there's a big one between Ryan and Arianna."

"Doesn't matter to him. He doesn't see it that way. He was cheering Ryan on, but he just doesn't feel like love is for him." Gavin pauses. "Not that he doesn't want it. He just wants Dallas to live life before getting saddled to anyone, least of all him."

"He needs to get his head out of his ass," Cole says.

Taylor chuckles. "I remember Ryan's battle. He was in love with Arianna for a lot longer than he admitted to himself or any of us. He felt like a pedophile because he fell for her before she was eighteen. She was still a kid in his mind. He questioned everything he did. He came to me one day and asked me if what he was doing with her could be deemed as grooming."

"Josh asked me that same question," I say. "I told him to get out of his fucking head."

"Pretty much what I told Ryan. Grooming is a lot different. There was never any kind of power and control with them. He always made sure she was free to make her own choices."

I nod at Taylor. "Same with Josh."

"I still say he needs to get his head out of his ass," Cole reiterates.

"One thing I know about Josh after all these years is he needs to fuck up, realize the fuck up, and learn from it. Then he'll fix it." Gavin starts driving after Josh, who is in the SUV in front of us, pulls away from the curb. "Never anything more or less. That's just Josh."

"Thank God he doesn't do that with missions," I say with a rare smile. I haven't smiled much at all since I lost Skyla.

I rest my arm on the window and drop my head in my hand as everyone goes silent. I lose myself in the dark landscape of Texas that we're speeding by. We're on our way back to Viper's Venom's compound where we're staying.

Of course that has to be another piece to this mysterious fucking puzzle. I let my head fall back against the headrest and close my eyes as I shake my head.

We're in Texas because someone from Viper's Venom saw Skyla. He followed her to an abandoned building, the warehouse we were just at. He fled back to the compound to let Blade, the president of this chapter of Viper's Venom, know what he saw. He took pics and everything, but he felt like he got spotted. He left because he didn't want to get caught by the large number of people he saw.

Blade mobilized people immediately. He got eyes on them and called Josh right away. We were already in the air by the time his team got to the warehouse. They observed. When they saw what looked to be them mobilizing to leave, they moved in.

Unfortunately, they were outmanned and outgunned. Lucky for them, we were almost there. When we showed up, the gunfight ended quickly, but it was far too late. During the chaos that ensued, Thurston escaped with Skyla. No one saw them leave. No one knew what direction they fled. All we knew was that a couple of his guys were killed, one was interrogated by Josh before he was shot between the eyes, courtesy of Josh Lucinio himself. We didn't get any useful information out of him at all.

The only thing we know is that whoever is leading this bullshit little biker gang has everyone scared to death of him. There's nothing about that statement that's good. It means people aren't afraid to die in order to keep secrets locked down. That never bodes well for any of the parties involved.

It also makes me quite curious about why. Why not give information about Skyla? Who is this leader, and why is he so powerful? Why is he feared so much? If the Crane and Lucinio mafias haven't been able to find him, what the fuck does that even mean? Is he more powerful than we are? Is that even a possibility?

When we pull into the compound and park in front of the main clubhouse, we all get out. Somberly, we all walk in. Everyone who's sitting in the clubhouse instantly stops talking and stares at us.

I follow Blade and Josh back to Blade's office. Gavin, Taylor, Damon, Cole, and Lance follow me. As soon as I close the door behind everyone, I collapse onto a couch in the back. Taylor sits next to me as everyone launches into new plans. Plans I simply have no energy to partake in.

"You have to focus on her being okay, Dane. Focusing on what you think is happening isn't going to help," Taylor says quietly as he sits down next to me.

I let out a breath. "How did you do it when Nikki was going through the shit she was? How did you stay away from her?"

He chuckles. "I didn't want to. I'll tell you that. Nic is a strong woman. So is Skyla. She has to be to survive what she did. Same with Nikki. It sucked being away from her, and I'll never say our situations are the same. They aren't. Not by a long shot. The only advice I can give is to trust her. Trust that she's surviving. We know she knows that we're looking for her. She's obviously trying to leave clues for us."

I nod. Every location we've been to has had one thing in common. A message that looks like a hand swiped through it. Maybe a foot.

"I just hate the fact that she felt she had to resort to this."

"Love is a fucked up thing, Dane. I wasn't too happy when I figured out Nicole's plan to catch her stalker. And I hated even more that she did it to protect me. She saw the toll it all took on me. Skyla is exactly the same. She saw you lying in a hospital bed recovering from being shot. She felt like she was directly responsible and could stop it from happening. Was it a stupid as hell decision on her part? Damn right, but when you look at this from her perspective, you'll see that she felt it was the right thing. This was the only option in her mind. The only way to keep the love of her life and the family she's grown to love from being hurt any further."

All I can do is nod because I know he's right. "I just keep thinking of those last words. That she'll love me until her last breath. It was like she was already giving up and accepting her fate. Like she knew she wouldn't survive this."

"I look at it like she was saying she'd fight for as long as she possibly could. Your love would be her strength."

I lift my hand and absently roll her ring she put in my hand between my fingers. I wear it on a chain around my neck and never take it off. When I felt it in my hand, I couldn't do anything but grip it as tightly as I could. It took me a while to figure out why she did it. I realized it's because Thurston never would've let her keep it.

I feel her love through it just as strongly as I feel her shoe digging into my right ass cheek. Like my love that she carries with her, her ring gives me the strength to keep pushing forward. Keep hoping.

"Thank you, Taylor. For everything, but especially for coming with me on all of these dead ends we find ourselves in."

He pats my knee and leans back on the couch. "You think I'm going to let my best friend do this without me? Fuck no. You've been with me through hell and back. May as well stick by your side and fight with you through it again. We've already been there, right? Pretty sure the devil fears us by this point. We might be the only fuckers who've dared to walk through his realm more than once."

I can't help but smile. "I think it's a good thing we're in good with him." I nod towards Josh. "Asshole killed the devil and took over."

Taylor barks out a laugh. I grin even wider as we both fall silent. I really am glad he's with me. Taylor Reddick might be the only one in this world who can get me to focus on the task at hand.

And that task is finding my wife.

Chapter Eighteen

☙ Skyla ❧

(Two Months Later)

Four months.

Four… long… months…

This was a mistake. I know that now. If I could take back this stupid, stupid decision, I would do it in a split second. I should've trusted Josh and the mafia. I should've stayed with Dane. I should've turned around and run to Racheal. I should've found a guard.

I should've…

Should've…

Should've…

Should've…

"You okay?" Aero asks me. He's a big guy. Really muscular and tall. And he's really fast on his bike. I don't know his real name. I just know what the other biker's call him.

He's been my saving grace since my very first second with him. He was the one who picked me up from the parking lot. As soon as we hit the street, he shouted back to me that I could trust him. I didn't believe him at all, but he's proven himself time and time again. Since that first day, he's treated me like a human, far better than Thurston has.

I didn't know it then, but he's the Vice President of this biker crew. I don't know who the president is, but whoever it is seems to be on his side because I've heard him reprimanding Thurston over the phone.

It just makes Thurston more and more irate, though. The few times he has gotten to me have been times when Aero wasn't here. Or when he was here but not anywhere near me. Close enough that he could hear me scream, though. He's always said if Thurston touches me to scream. He'd be here.

I still can't figure out why. He's still a bad guy. I know that. He's part of the Ruthless Warriors. I know from what Dane has said that the Ruthless Warriors are not the good guys in this equation. So, why Aero seems to be taking care of me is something I still haven't managed to figure out.

I glance at him as I stir the hamburger meat. I shrug. "I guess."

Aero is quiet for a while as I cook the meat. Finally, I hear him sigh. "I think we need something a little stronger than tacos for this conversation. I know something is on your mind." He gives me a side hug. "I'll be right back. I'm gonna grab some of the good whiskey from my room."

I chuckle. "I don't need whiskey. I need a hero."

"Whiskey." He walks quickly towards his bedroom.

I shake my head but let myself smile a little. I add some water to my cooked hamburger that I've cut up into pieces for the tacos. I add a seasoning packet and let it simmer as I warm the shells just a little.

My punishment for not looking at Thurston when he was speaking to me two days ago was that I couldn't eat anything. He also told me if I said a word to Aero, he'd make me pay. I believed him because he's found ways to inflict as much harm on me as possible. He never hits my face. Never chokes me. But he does other things.

Just like before.

I can't sit sometimes. My legs, butt, and arms are always bruised. Even if I scream out and Aero comes running, the damage has already been done. I don't know how high in the ranks Thurston is, but I know that he can break rules and get away with it. Nothing ever seems to happen to him despite Aero's warnings to back off me.

I still can't figure a lot of it out, but it's Aero's protectiveness that really confuses me.

I set the shells on the counter and turn back to the meat. Seeing it's done, I cover it and move it to a back burner that's not lit as I turn the one I was using off.

I can smell Thurston before I see him. Before I have a chance to react, his fist meets the back of my head. I fly forward barely missing the still hot burner and the pan with the meat in it. I instantly see stars and feel like I'm going to throw up. My knees buckle, but before I can fall to the ground, Thurston has his arms around me and is slamming me face first into a wall.

"I love when you disobey me," he growls against my neck before he licks it. I shudder. He slaps a hand over my mouth just as I'm about to scream. "Bite my hand. I fucking dare you." His voice is as dark as the most evil demon. I stay as still as possible and try not to cry. "Good girl," he growls. "What did I tell you about eating?" He tugs my hair with his free hand and holds me against the wall with his body. With his other hand still over my mouth, he slams my head into the wall. "Answer." He moves his hand back just a little bit but keeps a tight hold on my hair.

"N-not t-to…," I choke out. I'm not going to last much longer. My vision is darkening quickly. I'm going to pass out.

"Yet here you are. About to stuff your fucking face. Breaking my rule."

"What the ever living fuck do you think you're doing?" Like an avenging angel, Aero appears out of nowhere. I let out a relieved sob.

"Doesn't concern you, Aero. Walk away," Thurston growls.

"Not a chance, Shovelhead." Thurston's biker name. He hates it, but he's not the one who got to pick it. Everyone else did. He doesn't think it's cool. "Let her go before I make you pay the consequences." Aero's voice is so calm, but I can hear the edge behind it. I don't need to look to see Thurston shooting daggers at him.

"You gonna go running to daddy? Tell him all the bad shit I'm doing again? You fuckers wouldn't be here if not for me funding your little funhouse."

The next thing I know, Thurston is falling backwards, and I'm sinking to the floor. My hand flies to the back of my head. I don't know if he yanked out a fistful of my hair or not, but the stabbing pain I feel is overwhelming and briefly makes me forget about the agony of my head being slammed into the wall.

"For the record, asshole. She's making food for me. Now, get the fuck up and out of my face," Aero growls. I thought Thurston had a dangerous darkness. I was wrong. Aero is far more evil. His voice never portrays it, but it just did.

I don't dare look at either of them. Instead, I cower on the floor curled in the tightest ball, making myself the smallest I possibly can. Maybe neither of them will know I'm here anymore. Maybe they'll think I ran away. It's impossible for me to move. I'm frozen in fear, but maybe they won't notice me.

I keep my eyes squeezed shut and try to ignore the rapid beating of my own heart. I need to hear if they leave. I fight the rising nausea I'm sure is caused by the wall and the violent way I was slammed into it.

When I feel a hand on my shoulder, I nearly leap out of my skin, but I'm still too terrified to move a single inch. I keep my arms around my head. I stay on my side with my knees tucked as close to my chin as I can physically make them.

"It's me, Skyla," Aero's deep and somehow calming voice rumbles. His hand doesn't leave my shoulder. My brain can't decide if I'm safe or in danger. My body doesn't know if it wants to flee or fight, so it stays frozen solidly in place. "It's okay. I'm not going to hurt you. You know that." He gently squeezes my shoulder. "He's gone. I'll deal with him."

I swallow. Hard. "Why are you helping me?" I whisper. "Why have you helped me for all of this time, but not just taken me back home?"

"Come with me. Come to my room. We'll talk. I'll tell you everything I can."

It takes time for me to move, but Aero is beyond patient with me. I'm not sure why. When I do finally move, he helps me to my feet. "Thank you," I whisper when I'm finally on my feet.

He doesn't let me go. "Feeling okay?" He looks deep in my eyes. I can tell he's searching them for any kind of a sign of a concussion or problem. He's done it every time Thurston has put his hands on me.

"I feel a little sick. My head is pounding." I want to look down, but I don't. "I'm dizzy."

"Partially because you haven't eaten in two days, I'm sure." His eyes darken. "I'm sorry I didn't know about that. I'm even more sorry the person I left in charge of you didn't follow my orders."

My eyes widen slightly, but I'm left even more confused. "It's been four months, and I still don't understand any of this. I don't know why you're doing what you're doing. I don't understand why you leave people to watch over me. I don't deserve any of this... I belong to him." This time I do look down. I've felt very defeated for a long time.

"You don't belong to anyone but yourself, Skyla."

I sniffle. "I just want to go home."

"I know it's not much coming from a complete stranger who's anything but a good guy, but trust me when I say I'll get you out of here. I made you a promise. I'm working on it. I need things in place first. I need to be able to protect myself from the fallout. I'm close, Skyla. I promise."

I can't help but notice how nervously he's looking around as he talks to me. How his voice is a gentle whisper. So, I nod and silently help him gather the food that somehow stayed intact. Even the meat seems warm. We work side by side to build our tacos. Aero grabs drinks for us and the bottle of whiskey he grabbed along with two glasses. We put the food on a serving tray, and he follows me to his room.

We put everything down, and I crawl into his bed. I'm freezing. It's cold here, and I'm not allowed to wear anything less than a flimsy, almost see-through tank top with barely there silk shorts. I'm never warm. We're somewhere in the mountains at some hideout. I was never privy to where, but if I had to guess, it would be Mount Everest just because of how cold and windy it is.

Seconds after disappearing into the bathroom, Aero comes back out with a cloth and towel. He sits next to me and gently cleans my face. I'm not sure what it looks like, but there must be some kind of wound on it. It stings a little, but I've started to realize I'm just becoming numb.

Except to the cold.

I shiver a little. I don't think I've stopped shivering for months, save for brief periods of time where Aero hides me for a while so I can warm up. Or when he intentionally builds a fire in the fireplace and invites me to sit with him and the guys. It pisses Thurston off, but I'm starting to think he likes doing that.

Without saying a word, Aero locks his bedroom door and walks back to the bathroom. He comes back out and grabs a sweatshirt for me. I look at it longingly and practically throw it on like it's the only piece of clothing I've ever had.

"We need to keep it down," Aero says quietly. He sets the tray of food on my lap and crawls into the bed with me. He's wearing sweatpants and a t-shirt. I don't understand how he isn't cold.

"Okay."

When he's settled next to me and finds a movie that neither of us will be watching, I set the tray between us. I don't even care that it's probably cold right now. I haven't eaten anything in a couple of days, but before that, I've eaten hardly anything at all in weeks. I didn't know the amount of weight I lost until Aero pointed it out to me.

I'm grateful to him for a lot of things, the protection mostly. While he's not able to stop it all, he's kept me alive this long. I don't doubt that Thurston would have killed me long ago. One of the biggest things, though, is that he gave me my own room with a lock on the door right next to his. Thurston was beyond pissed, but I could never thank Aero enough for doing it. I don't want to think of the things that would be happening to me if I were forced into a bedroom with Thurston.

"I have a very thin line to walk," Aero begins as we both eat. "There are a lot of things going on that cross my lines and come up against my morals. My lines are thin, and my morals are almost non-existent, but there are a few things that bother me. One of them involves kids. The other involves blatant disrespect. And the last one involves women. When I first got into this, I was fed a lot of bullshit. Over the years, I've caught lies. Way more deceit than I can even explain. I honestly don't know if I would've given a shit until about six months ago."

I finish off my first taco. "That... was a couple of months before..." I trail off and focus on my next taco.

"Yep. Before you." Silence hangs between us for a few minutes as we both concentrate on the food. Finally, Aero takes a deep breath. "I started questioning shit I shouldn't have. Prez started threatening my wife and daughter."

My head snaps to him. I ignore the dizziness it causes and focus completely on what he just said. "You have a family?" I ask just as quietly as he's talking.

He nods and grins. "I do. They're my entire life. I have a little house on our compound back home. But since I started getting suspicious of shit, I've been being sent on missions that keep me far away from them. My wife says she's doing good. Everything is fine. But she feels Prez is getting a little unhinged lately. I told her to come here, but he stopped that. He's trying to play protector. He's saying it's too dangerous. He doesn't think they should be out here. Things could turn ugly. They could get hurt. That shit might fly, except I know he's using them as leverage to keep me playing his game. He doesn't know just how much I know, and I intend to keep it that way. I'll just play dumb Vice Prez and follow all the rules like a good boy. But I've got things in the works to take him down. I just need my wife and daughter out of harm's way."

I nibble my lip. "I…" My head is spinning, but not from the injuries.

"You're wondering why I haven't gone to Josh."

I look at him a little bewildered. "I mean, kinda, yeah."

"The answer is, I am. I am going to go to him. But I have to make sure I have a plan for them. I need to get them out. I'm sure he could help, but I don't trust anyone in this crew. I can't tell them to watch for him because the phones are tapped. I'm not supposed to know that, but I heard him talking to Thurston about it. Thurston's a fucking cocky moron and had the damn phone on speaker. I have to figure out a way to get them a warning before I call in the calvary. Beyond that, though, I also need some information I can bring to Josh. I have some things, but I don't have it all. I want him to have a full rundown on some of the shit going on. I can get that for him, but I can't if I'm not in good with Prez. I also didn't have an in with Josh. When Thurston got your call, I demanded he let me get you and convinced him that there would be guards all over him if he did it."

I nod slowly and finish off my last taco. "You're right. I need a shot for this one."

Aero chuckles and pours some in a glass. Probably equal to two shots. It takes everything in me to sip and not slam. Probably not a good thing to do with a concussion, if I have one anyway. Pretty sure I do. I swirl the amber liquid in the glass as what I drank burns its way down my throat.

"I'm your in."

"You're my in with Josh, but that's not why you've been stuck here for four months, Skyla. I promise you that. It all has to do with me needing to get information while working on a way to get my wife a message. I need my family safe. They're my number one priority. I have to be able to take care of them. I need them okay even if it means I won't be there. If I can get them under Lucinio Mafia's protection, I don't care if Josh kills me or your husband throws me in jail for the rest of my life. Truth is, when I finish my story and hand over all the documentation they need, your husband will have enough to lock me up and throw away the key. I'd never see the light of day again. And that's only if Josh doesn't get his hands on me first."

I shake my head. "They're not like that," I say quietly. "They protect the good guys."

"I'm far from a good guy, Skyla."

I shake my head. "I see the good. So will they. And if they don't, you can count on me to make them. It's the least I can do for you for all of your help. I'd be dead if not for you."

"Well, I appreciate that."

A comfortable silence falls over us both. We both finish our whiskey. Aero cleans everything up as I sink into the warm, thick blankets that I don't have the luxury of in my bedroom. Not that I don't have blankets. I have one. And it's thin. I haven't said anything to Aero because Thurston said he'd lock me in the basement with nothing at all if I did that. The basement is soundproof. No one would hear me scream.

Aero climbs back into his bed and shuts off the lights. "New rule. After what happened tonight, your room is now this one." He wraps an arm around me, and I sink into him gratefully as I cry quietly.

All of the sadness, hurt, anger, frustration, and relief come out in near silent sobs. Aero says absolutely nothing. He just hugs me, and I didn't realize just how much I needed that.

For the first time, I let myself fully trust him. I put my entire life into his hands not because I don't have a choice, but because I truly believe he'll get me out of here.

That he'll get me back home...

Chapter Nineteen

🍒 Dane 🍒

(Two Months Later)

I pull my car into Lance and Damon's driveway. I got a call from Lance a little while ago saying to come by. It's important. He wouldn't give me details. All he said was to come in. Door is open. I'm assuming it has something to do with some information I wanted him to pull for me about another case I'm working on that has nothing to do with Skyla or the Ruthless Warriors.

At least, I didn't think it did at first. I should've known better. Every fucking case my team has been handed lately has come back to the Ruthless Warriors. It pisses me off because I feel like it's leading us all further from Skyla. It's a distraction.

The problem the Ruthless Fuck-ups didn't count on is that I've learned a thing or two over the years. I can pick up on distractions from bigger things from ten miles away. I might think in the beginning it's unrelated, but I always end up finding a connection quickly, if there is one. It's part of the reason I'm in the position I'm in and leading my own team.

The other part, of course, is because my brother needed someone on his side that Taylor is for Ryan. Someone who can get him information if he needs it and can lead a team capable of helping him if he needs it. Some call it a cover up. I've always called it protecting the good deeds of some vigilantes. A few good people who sometimes aren't that good who can do things those of use who wear a badge can't.

Fucked up, but necessary.

It's the connection I think I found to Ruthless Warriors in my most recent case that I called Lance in on. I needed him to track a hunch. The case surrounds a bunch of younger men who have gone missing. All have rap sheets a mile long. I've dealt with several of them myself. It's mostly drugs and car thefts.

Then, motorcycles started going missing from dealerships, and known drug dealers began turning up dead. That's when I landed on the conclusion that it's all connected. And it's why I got Lance involved.

As Lance requested, I walk in and close the door behind me. The first thing I see is Damon lying on the couch wearing jeans and no shirt. That's no surprise. What is surprising is what's on the TV. I glance around and see his teenage daughter, Rosie, nowhere in sight.

I clear my throat as I look down at him with an amused smile. "Tangled? Like... the Disney movie?"

Damon narrows his eyes and points at me. "Tell... no... one...," he growls threateningly.

I bite my lip to keep from grinning and raise my hands in mock surrender. "Where's your better half?"

He points down the hall. "Office. Enter at your own risk. He hasn't slept."

It's my turn to narrow my eyes, but I head for the office anyway. The door is open, and it's quiet. I take that as a good sign. When I step in, Lance is sitting behind the desk with his nose behind three computer screens. I don't need to look at any of them to know that they all show something different, and he probably has several tabs open on each one all doing different things at the same time. I sit down on the couch and wait him out.

A few minutes later, his head pops up. "You're right. It's connected to Ruthless Warriors. I pulled footage from the dealerships the bikes were stolen from. I followed traffic cams all the way to this little shop at the edge of the North side. I had to pull a few systems from some buildings, but they clearly take them to this shop. I did some digging. The shop is owned by Maxwell Thurston. I don't know how the fuck he thought I wouldn't figure that out."

I shake my head. "He's leaving names that are just too easy. There has to be a bigger game at play here."

"Or he just doesn't care. He thinks because he has money, he's untouchable. It makes him cocky. And that cockiness causes him to make mistakes."

I ponder that for a few moments but don't get a chance to respond before Josh strides into the office with Damon, now wearing a t-shirt, Gavin, and Cole right behind him. I raise an eyebrow as everyone sits down in silence. Lance is the only one who doesn't focus on Josh standing in the middle of the room. Almost like he already knows what's happening.

Confirming my suspicions, Lance hands Josh a stack of papers. "We have some information on where Skyla might be," Josh says while leafing through the papers.

I perk up at the statement and glance over my shoulder when I hear someone walking into the office. "Just a sec, man. I'm putting you on speaker," Alec says as he walks into the room. He looks at Josh. "This is big." He puts his phone on speaker and turns it up so we all can hear. "Aero, I have you on speaker. You've got the ears of me and the leader of Lucinio Mafia. Tell him what you just told me."

Lance stops tapping at his keys and focuses solely on Alec. Josh raises an eyebrow as he looks down at the phone. Me, Gavin, Damon, and Cole all stare with our mouths partially open. I'm probably the only one holding my breath. I want Josh to continue with what he was about to say, but whatever Alec has must be big if he's involving us.

"Are you sure this is a good idea, Prez? Because I'm fucked up over this," the voice on the other line says. Aero. That must be his biker name. He must be Viper's Venom if he's calling Alec 'Prez'.

"I'm sure. You trust me. I trust them," Alec says.

I hear a deep breath. "Okay. Mr. Lucinio, I'm on a burner phone. My name is Aero. I'm not divulging my real name. Not yet. I need your help. I need your assurance you'll help me get the fuck out of here. I have Skyla with me."

"What?" I blurt out with wide eyes as I stand. I look at Josh frantically.

"Who was that?" Aero asks, panicked. "Ace? Who the fuck was that?"

"Calm down, Aero. It was Dane. Skyla's husband. He's part of the Lucinio Mafia. The second and third in command are here as well as their tech guy. Dane is here with his Sergeant."

"Fuck, man. I'm having a fucking heart attack."

"You need to trust me. I got your back." Alec looks at Josh. "Aero is at a villa in Glattalpsee."

"Switzerland?" Josh asks.

"Yes, sir. We're in the mountains," Aero says. I just stare at the phone as I plan out how to get my girl back. My head is spinning. "I'll send the coordinates, but I need your help. My wife and daughter were moved to what's supposed to be an undisclosed location. I know the coordinates. I'll send them to you. But I need your assurance she's safe. They'll kill her." There's shuffling. "I have to go. Now. I'll text the coordinates to her." He hangs up before I can question him.

"Fuck!" I push my fingers through my hair as I growl. "Who is this motherfucker? Who the fuck does he think he is to keep Skyla away from me?"

"There's more to the story," Josh says. He puts a hand on my shoulder. "Sit. Let Alec explain. I doubt he'd come here without something more than that. Obviously, he trusts this Aero person."

I sit, but it's more because if I don't, my legs are going to give out. I lean back against the couch. "I'm going to either pass out or lose my fucking mind. I'm on the line."

"Well, maybe this will help," Alec begins. "Aero. He's the VP of Ruthless Warriors. He called me a little while ago. Said he was on a burner phone. He knows his phone is being tapped, and so is his wife's. He got her a message a little while ago through someone he trusts. Someone he's been testing for a while. It's this same person who told him that his wife got moved. She told him where. She took pictures."

"Give me the coordinates," Lance says. "I can use satellites to observe."

"Fuck, lets not get the State Department up our ass," Cole rumbles.

"I have my own access." Lance grins and winks. Cole stares in open-mouthed shock while Alec gives him the coordinates and a picture of Aero's wife and daughter.

"He says he has a lot of information for us on the Ruthless Warriors. Enough to take them the fuck down once and for all," Alec continues. "Also of interest. He called me because he found out the leader of the Ruthless Warriors used to be a member of Viper's Venom. He went rogue." Alec meets Josh's eyes.

Gavin leans forward. "When."

"About the time we were in Texas," Alec finishes.

"Son of a bitch," Josh growls.

"I already called Blade," Alec says. "That's not even all. They've been recruiting, but the people they're recruiting are in their twenties."

"And they all have a rap sheet a mile long, steal bikes from dealerships, and take them to a chop shop owned by the RW," I finish.

Alec blinks. "How the fuck did you know that?"

"Because I'm working the case. Lance just confirmed all of that for me. The chop shop is owned by Maxwell Thurston. He sucks at coming up with alias names. Lance thinks he just doesn't give a shit. He has the money and is cocky as fuck."

"I'm with Lance on that one," Gavin says as he looks at Josh. "I say we take out the chop shop. That's where the recruits will be. They'll be busily cleaning vins while mechanics are making the bikes unrecognizable. Probably painting and customizing."

Alec shakes his head. "No. They're staying at an old warehouse Thurston had fixed up. Aero confirmed that. I sent some guys to check it out."

"We take the shop and the warehouse at the same time," Josh says.

My heart leaps in my throat. "Josh, no. Fuck no."

Josh holds up a hand. "Let me finish. We take them out at the same time. A coordinated attack. But we do it at the same time we take his wife and daughter. Which will be the same time we get Skyla. We'll need to do everything here at night, which means we'll be grabbing Skyla in broad daylight."

I stand up again and rub my head as I pace. After a few moments, I stop in front of Josh. "I don't care what we do, but we need her back. It's been six months. I don't know if this is a trick or if she's still alive. How the fuck do we know if we can trust this person?"

Josh looks at Alec. "Good question."

Alec shrugs. "We don't. But he admitted that. He's aware he needs to earn the trust. He's also aware that when you and Dane get your hands on him, he's either going to jail or hell. All he cares about is his wife and daughter and making sure Skyla is out of there. Truthfully, he's risking his life. Gotta give him credit for that. But when it comes down to it, everything he said can be either proven or disproven. We have Lance for that."

"I don't like the fact that he hung up like that," I tell Alec. "I need something. I need assurance. I need to see Skyla. Hear her. I have to know she's okay. I don't want to walk into a fucking ambush, and I want to know she's safe."

"I know, Dane. When I talked to him earlier, he assured me he'd get pics. When he calls back, and I trust that he will, I'll give him your number. He needs to be safe. And we need him safe because from what he said, he's the only thing standing in the way of Skyla and Thurston. He's been protecting her since day one."

"Then why the fuck didn't he call earlier?" I roar in frustration.

"Because of his wife, man. His family. He has a little girl and a wife to think about, too. He knew damn well he couldn't just come to us with nothing. He's given me some stuff that I'm here to give to Lance to look into. I've looked myself, and shit checks out. But I know I can't go as deep as he can. What I do know is that he's called from two different numbers so far. That means he's destroying phones and covering his tracks. He's smart."

"I'm not fucking trusting a word until I see her," I growl.

"Well, then trust this," Lance says, turning a screen. "His text to Alec with the coordinates also gave detailed information about the layout and size of the house as well as how many guards there are. It checks out. The house his wife is at is way back in the sticks of Texas near Waco. The address is on the mailbox at the end of a long driveway. There are four guards, just like the text said. Details of the house check out. And there are two females inside. Both of them look exactly like the picture he sent."

"How the fuck do you see all of that from satellite images?" Damon asks in disbelief. I love how he's always so surprised at the things his husband can do.

Lance chuckles. "I know that's not doubt in your sexy voice. But to answer, you know how GPS works? Same technology."

I chuckle. "But you can see in people's houses."

Lance grins and puts a finger to his lips. "Shh… don't tell anyone. Besides, with great power comes great responsibility and all that shit."

"Yeah, but if you can do that, imagine what the Government can," I retort.

"Let's hope they ain't." Lance turns his screen. "Truthfully, you need more technology than what a satellite has. More programs. But imagine this. We have technology to see details of other planets, including the rings around Saturn. That's hundreds of millions of miles away. Seems a little unlikely we can't make out details on our very own planet when the furthest satellite from us is only just over twelve-hundred miles away." Lance starts writing something down. "When he sends those other coordinates, let me know."

"You got it," Alec says. "I'll stay in the compound tonight. Got a room for me?"

Josh chuckles. "You know your room is always open."

I take a breath as we all follow Josh out, except for Lance and Damon. There's no way I'm not going to be involved in the planning stages. And I'm sure as hell going to be there when we rescue my girl.

"Josh," I say as soon as we get outside.

He turns to me. "Yeah?"

"You know I'm not staying behind."

"I didn't think you would be."

I nod, a little relieved that he's on my side. "Think I can stay with you? I don't want to miss anything if he calls."

"I'll make you up a room. Grab some stuff for a few days. I'm sure you aren't going to want to miss any part of the planning."

I shake my head. "Not a chance."

I head for my truck and jump in. My house is only a couple of houses down, but I don't want to just leave my vehicle here.

I quickly drive home, grab some stuff I'll need for a few days, and drive over to Josh's. I want to have my vehicle close if I need it.

For the first time in months, I feel like we're getting close. I don't know who this Aero person is. I still don't know if he can be trusted. I hope that he's really on our side and protecting Skyla.

Tears sting my eyes for the millionth time over the past six months, but this time. It's different. This time they're filled with both adrenaline and hope.

I'm coming, baby. Fuck, just hold on for me, Sky.

Chapter Twenty

☙ Skyla ❧

(One Week Later)

"Trust me," Aero says to me. "It's a lot safer for you down here."

"You don't understand," I whisper. "This is my biggest fear. Thurston has threatened me for so long about locking me down here." I cling to his arm and stick as close to his body as I possibly can. I don't even care that it probably seems weird that I'm practically trying to climb him. "Please don't make me stay down here. I'll be safe in your room."

"Skyla, I can't guarantee that." He shakes his head. "What I can promise is that it won't be long." He keeps his voice low. It's dark. I can barely make him out even though I'm clinging to him. He's less than centimeters away from me.

I sniffle. "I c-can't. I can't d-do this."

"You can. You need to be strong. This is almost over, Skyla. You've held out for this long. This isn't going to be your breaking point." He kneels down with me and settles me on the cushion of blankets from his bed. "You have a sweatshirt. Sweats. You have warm socks with your shoes. And you have this heavy blanket to wrap yourself in." He takes out his phone and dials a number. With the dim light, I can see he looks up the stairs as he hands me the phone. I take it and put it up to my ear.

"Tell me we're ready to do this, man. I can't handle it anymore."

"Dane…," I whisper, my voice catching.

"Oh fuck, baby. Fuck. Are you okay? What's going on?" The hard edge to his voice is gone, and I almost lose it.

I swallow down the lump in my throat instead. This is the second time I've gotten to talk to him, and it's just as heartbreaking and relieving as the first time. "It's okay. I'm in the basement."

"Good. Good, baby. We have a team going straight to the basement entrance. I'll be with them. As soon as Aero gives us the go ahead."

"I'm scared. I'm so scared. It's dark down here. It's cold. Thurston has been threatening to lock me down here to keep me in line ever since we got here."

"Baby, it's okay. I promise it's okay. Aero has you in the safest location. We don't know the kind of hell that's going to be unleashed in that house. I need you to be brave for me, sweet girl."

"Just tell me you love me again. Tell me you're coming for me," I whisper.

"I love you, Skyla. And I'm fucking coming for you."

I take a breath and let the words sink it. "I love you," I choke out over the sob that escapes, even though I try to fight it. "I love you so much."

"I need to get back up there, Skyla," Aero rumbles.

I close my eyes and nod again. "Okay," I say to him. "Dane?"

"Yeah, baby?"

"Tell Josh to show no mercy," I growl low.

"No mercy will be given, beautiful."

I hand the phone back to Aero refusing to say goodbye. It's not goodbye. I'll never say that word again for as long as I live.

Aero hangs up the phone and adjusts the blanket around me. "It won't be long. Just think of Dane. Think of his voice. Pretend you're anywhere with him but here." He moves the blanket so it's over my head. "If you need to hide in the blanket and use my scent, do it. Just imagine anywhere but here."

I nod and burrow. "Aero?" I say as he stands.

"Yeah?"

"Thank you."

"I'll see you out there."

I nod. "I'll see you out there."

I listen to him walk away. He glides as quietly as he can up the stairs. I can tell he pauses at the top and listens before he cracks the door and slips out. The basement isn't soundproof like Thruston told me. Aero assured me of that. He said he could hear me if I screamed.

Him slipping out is the last bit of light I see. There are no windows down here. The air is stale and stagnant. It's freezing cold. Colder than I imagined it would be in the first place. I thought maybe the snow on the ground outside would help insulate the basement a little bit. Maybe it is. Maybe it would be colder without the snow, but it's still far colder than I anticipated it would be.

I shiver a little before burrowing deeper into the thick blanket. I didn't realize it, but on top of the comforter around me is another blanket. It feels like wool. So I tuck myself more into it and lean my back against the support beam that Aero positioned me next to. I fully immerse myself into the blankets and close my eyes. It makes it darker, but I don't care. My breath is warm and helps keep me warm as I insulate.

To anyone who sees me right now, I might just look like a pile of blankets. They wouldn't be able to see any part of me. If they look close enough and listen, they would see and hear me breathing, but nothing more. I'm okay with that.

Taking Aero's advice, I imagine myself safe at home with Dane. It's the same thought that has kept me going. Dane's arms wrapped around me. Dane whispering he loves me. Dane promising to always protect me and doing just that.

I'm sure it's been a million times, but I once again think how stupid it was to do what I did. Aero has talked to me about it over and over again. I understand that I was absolutely in a panic. Anyone would be seeing their husband lying in a hospital bed unmoving like that. It's understandable that my thought process went the way it did. I viewed Thurston as the threat. And I knew exactly how to eliminate the threat to the man I love; the family that means the world to me.

But I still can't help thinking that it was the worst decision in the history of decisions. Okay, maybe not all decisions… But it has to be at the top. I put myself through all of this, but what's worse to me is that I put Dane through so much stress and worry. I put Josh in a position where he has to put things aside to find me and rescue me. Those things are unforgivable to me.

I shake my head and focus my attention back on Dane. His body wrapped around as we watch a movie while eating popcorn with M&Ms is one of my favorite ways to calm down. It always leads to him nibbling on my neck and telling me I'm a better snack than the M&M popcorn. Then he always makes me forget what movie we're even watching as his hand slides down my body and slips into my panties. He always makes me come a couple of times before he takes it all home. By the time we both finish, we're sweaty and writhing messes.

I smile to myself and bite my lip as I let the fantasy continue. Anything to keep my mind off the fact that I'm alone in a freezing cold, damp, and dark basement. That my life is literally hanging on the words of one man who has admitted that he's not a good guy. While I see good qualities about him, I know that he's right. He's told me about a lot of bad things he's done during one of our late night talks.

It doesn't matter much to me, though. For the past couple of months, Thurston hasn't been able to get near me. Much to his dismay. He doesn't like that I have the protection of someone with more power in the Ruthless Warriors than he has. He hates that he can't just throw money at the problem and solve it that way. Aero protecting me is a problem to him.

It's made him more and more unhinged. He screams and yells a lot, but it's directed at everyone, including the leader. He doesn't like being silenced. He hates feeling powerless. I can't be sure, but I think he's lost access to his money. I thought I heard Aero talking to someone about locking Thurston's accounts. I never asked him about it. I'm not certain I really care. I know Thurston hasn't been the one running his company the whole time we've been here. I don't know who is, though.

Suddenly, I hear yelling above me.

Stomping.

Shooting.

Screaming.

I wrap myself up tighter and cry quietly. I'm positive Josh is up there and has everything completely under his control, but I worry about him and his team. I worry about Aero. What if they don't recognize him?

What if they don't know what he looks like at all? What if they take him for one of the others and shoot him?

Seconds after the chaos above me starts, I hear a loud bang. It sounds like a door is exploding off its hinges. I barely contain the scream. I wrap myself tighter and keep my eyes squeezed shut. My heart is in my stomach. My stomach is in my mouth. I'm certain my lungs have collapsed because they aren't expanding with air anymore.

"Skyla!" Dane shouts. My eyes fly open. Even with the blankets over my head, everything seems to get lighter.

"Dane?" I squeak out. I scramble to remove the blankets from my head.

"Stay down!" he commands. I stop mid motion. I can't help the scream that escapes from my throat when I hear more shooting. Only this time, it's so much louder. There's no denying it's happening in the basement.

As quickly as it started, it stops. For a few moments, it doesn't seem like anything is moving, including the air. Everything is so silent, I could hear a teardrop fall. I don't dare breathe.

"He's down," someone says.

I let out a small gasp and swallow the sob down. "D-Dane. P-please s-say it's not Dane...," I whisper.

I feel someone kneel next to me. With gentle hands that leave me with a small twinge of hope, someone removes the blankets from over my head. As soon as light hits my eyes, I squint. It takes several moments for my eyes to adjust, but when they do, the first thing I see is the face of the man who has kept me going for so long.

Dane.

"Am I dreaming...?" I ask afraid to actually think he's really in front of me.

He shakes his head slowly with a soft smile that radiates so much love. His eyes are watery and shine with all of the emotions we both are feeling. It's all it takes for me to fight my way out of the blankets and launch myself into his arms.

I burst into tears of relief when his arms circle around me. He hugs me tight as he stands. He kisses me long and deeply before he bends and lifts me off the ground. I burrow my face into his neck and breathe him in. He carries me up the stairs into the bitter, early morning cold, but I don't feel it. All I feel is him. His warmth and strength radiate through me, penetrating me as deeply as his love and warming my soul.

"I need to get him to the hospital right now, Josh. Can we get the helicopter up here?"

My eyes fly open. My head snaps towards the sound of Dr. Freeman's voice. "What? Who? Who got hurt?" My eyes lock onto the body that Josh and Gavin are carrying. Josh has the body's arms. Gavin has the legs. "No!" I scream, attempting to launch out of Dane's arms. "No! Aero!" I shriek the second I realize who it is. I push at Dane, but he only holds me tighter.

"Shh... Baby, he'll be okay," Dane says in my ear. His arms are locked around me, and I'm too weak to fight him off.

"Aero!" I shout again as Dane walks closer. As soon as we reach him, he lets me down. "Oh God, Aero. What happened to you?"

He doesn't answer. His eyes are closed. There's blood dripping from somewhere onto the pure white, snow-covered ground. My shoes aren't that great. I can feel the wet snow seeping into them and soaking my socks, but all I care about is Aero.

"We found him in the kitchen. He gave us the signal. We entered within seconds," Gavin says. "We think Thurston hit him with a pan just after he gave us the signal." He clears his throat and looks down as Dr. Freeman works to bandage Aero's head. "We think he hit him twice."

"Oh my God." I shakily take one of Aero's cold hands dangling at his side.

"Dane, call in the helicopter. Pilot is on standby."

"On it." Dane takes out his phone and does as Josh commanded.

"Damon!" Josh barks. "On the other side of the SUV! We need to get him inside so Freeman can work!"

"On it, boss!" Damon jogs to the other side of the SUV just as Aero's eyes start to open.

He squeezes my hand weakly. "Sky," he whispers.

I force the tears to stay away. I need to be strong. "It'll be okay, Aero... You're in good hands."

His smile is soft as he closes his eyes again. "Stay."

I jerk my head to Josh in a panic. Aero's grip weakens even more. "Josh, I -"

"I know," Josh says.

"Get in on the other side. I'll need you to hold his head for me," Dr. Freeman says as he stands. I don't hesitate to do exactly what he says. I run to the other side.

"Hang on, sweetheart," Damon rumbles. "We need to get him in first."

"Heli is three minutes out! He was already in the air," Dane says.

"Never mind getting him in," Dr. Freeman says. "Jackets. His body temp isn't regulating with him in this state."

No one hesitates to take off their coats as I run back to Aero. Josh and Gavin adjust their grips with the added weight of the extra warmth. We can hear the helicopter and are looking up at the bright sky. As I hold Aero's hand, Dane wraps himself around me.

"You're going with him," Josh says to me. "Dane can go, too. He can help Doc while you're buckled in the front. You need to get checked out."

I stay focused on Aero's pale face, but I nod. "Okay."

Josh barks out more orders at some of his guards before he turns back to Damon. "Damon! You and Lance grab some lights for the helicopter to help him land! There's some lights in the back of all the SUVs!"

"Got it!" Lance calls. They both run to the back of an SUV. Seconds later, they're guiding the helicopter to the ground with bright red lights.

The wind from the blades whips my hair around my face, but my focus is on Aero. I know I'm okay. Dane is here. I know I'm safe. My ordeal is over, but his is just beginning.

Swiftly, we hurry to load him in the helicopter. Dane and the doctor settle in the back as Josh buckles me in beside the pilot.

"This is Tanner," Josh says loud enough for me to hear over the roar of the whirring blades. "He's a former Navy SEAL. He's flown about anything you can think of during his time in the military. He did a lot of extra training. You're safe."

I nod in gratitude. Josh is very good about reading people. He must have known I was terrified being this vulnerable with someone I'd never met. Even with Dane here easing my fears, there was still some lingering.

"Get him stable enough to fly home!" Josh says to Dr. Freeman. "Work miracles, Doc!" Josh closes the door and slides the one in back shut.

Tanner hands me a headset. I put it on as he signals. Without saying a word, he starts the takeoff. I turn and focus on Dr. Freeman and Dane working on a barely conscious Aero.

I just want us all to get home safely and together.

Aero included.

Chapter Twenty One

🍒 Dane 🍒

(Three Weeks Later)

I kiss Skyla's neck as I pass her to get to the fridge. She smiles up at me adoringly, her eyes glowing like a diamond. I grin and grab the strawberry wine I have chilling. I've discovered that while she doesn't drink a lot, strawberry wine is her favorite. Specifically, Perrier-Jouet Rose Belle Epoque. I'm never without a bottle.

"Do you really think Aero is going to make it?" she asks as she finishes cutting up some strawberries.

I nod as I close the fridge. I set the bottle in the ice bucket and fill it with ice as I stand next to her. "I trust what Doc said. He must be doing pretty well if they're flying home right now."

She sighs and sets the knife she's using down slowly as she looks up at me. "I just... feel so bad leaving him there. He's alone."

I kiss her forehead. "Sweet girl, he's not alone. He's talked to you every single day. He's talked to his family. Dr. Freeman is with him. Alec is there with him with a few of his guys. He's got guards all over the place.

Someone is in his room at all times. He's doing really well considering the injuries."

"I know, but I promised I'd stay with him."

I turn to her and take her in my arms. "Skyla, he understands. Seeing you on FaceTime and Skype and everything is good for him. And he's seeing his wife and daughter every single day." I sway gently with her as I hug her tight.

"I'm just worried."

I kiss her temple. "You got really close to him, didn't you?" I know the answer. Over the past three weeks, she's told me everything that happened while she was being held captive.

"He kept me alive," she whispers. Words she's told me more times than I can count. I kept her going, I kept her alive just as he did. My memory and him physically putting himself between her and Thurston.

"I'll never be more grateful to anyone for that," I whisper back. Words I've told her a thousand times since I got her back. "You'll see him in the morning, baby. They're landing around three in the morning. He'll be staying with Dr. Freeman through his recovery. And his family is there already. He'll be set." I smile and pull away slowly but keep her in my arms. "So, how about we finish our snacks and sit down to watch those movies we picked out?"

That earns me a sweet and excited smile. "I still can't believe you've never seen *Geostorm*."

I laugh as we both turn to finish our movie binging snacks. "I can't believe you've never seen *Wedding Crashers*. You've missed out."

She giggles as she puts the strawberries on the divided serving platter. There are several different sections she can put stuff in. It's her favorite platter I own. She loves it so much that she bought two more. This one holds green olives, black olives, baby dill pickles, a variety of cheese, cream cheese fruit dip, strawberries, bananas, and grapes. In a second one, smaller than the other, she's put turkey, chicken, ham, and a couple sections of Wheat Thins and Ritz crackers.

To top it all off, in the large bowl in front of me is salted popcorn with peanut and regular M&Ms. It might be one of my personal favorite snacks. Especially when it's extra buttery and salty. Not that I don't end up spending a little extra time in the gym, but it's definitely worth it because I get to spend all that time eating it with her.

We carry all the snacks and wine to our den. It's our favorite place to watch movies and just chill out because it's one of the cozier rooms in the house. It's the only room with a fireplace, and she loves that. She has a little nook where she can read and look out at the lake.

After we're settled and *Geostorm* is playing, I spread her favorite fleece blanket over us. Neither of us know why she loves it so much. It's just a large, dark red blanket, but it's the one she always reaches for when she wants to snuggle.

I put an arm around her and pull her close as we both dig into our spread. No words are spoken. They're not needed. Sometimes, we both just have to feel each other and be in the presence of one another to be at peace.

Aero did have a lot of injuries. We're not sure what exactly happened, and he doesn't remember it all, but we think he was hit with a heavy pan, once in the back of the head, once in the face, and more than a few times in the back, stomach, and side. He's currently having a lot of memory issues. He's told Alec a few things, but he knows it's not everything.

He had a flash drive and a laptop. Both were smashed to hell. I doubt Robby or Lance will be able to recover anything on either of them, but I'm not so sure it matters. The things he has remembered have checked out. Lance has been able to corroborate pretty easily.

Not that all of his memory is wiped. He remembers his wife and daughter. He remembers Skyla. He remembers bits and pieces of many different things. Even conversations he's had with Skyla. As soon as she fills in the rest, it all comes back to him, and even a little more of something related to the conversation.

Of course, brains work in mysterious ways. Sometimes, nothing she says triggers him. It frustrates him. He has good and bad days, but he just wants to be completely healed.

Thurston on the other hand… Well, that fucker is never going to be able to touch Skyla or anyone else again. Aimee felt a lot better about moving into Skyla's penthouse as soon as she found out Thurston was dead. When we were going down the stairs to get Skyla, Thurston had somehow escaped the raid and was running down the stairs from the house to the basement.

The second he saw me, he pointed his gun at Skyla. I wasn't the only one who took the shot, but damn did it feel good seeing his body riddled with several bullet holes. He never got a shot off. It's the one thing Skyla hasn't asked about, and I haven't brought up. She's satisfied enough just knowing he's dead.

Once *Geostorm* finishes, I select *Wedding Crashers*. It's one of my favorites, so when Skyla enjoys it as much as me, I find myself falling more and more in love with her. As if that's even possible.

Once it finishes, Skyla looks up at me. "That was such a beautiful movie. I don't know why I've never seen it."

I lean in and kiss her softly. "You've been deprived of one of the finer things in life." I grin and start picking up the remains of our snacks. There's still a half bottle of wine, but we did pretty good about eating all the food.

Skyla giggles as she gets up to help. "I think we need a *Fifty Shades* kind of night."

"Fuck that idea right into the red room."

She giggles again. "You need a red room."

I laugh. "The room wasn't even really red. It was red with some black and some mirrors and other bullshit. Obviously the person who wrote that has never actually seen a red room."

Her eyes widen. "Have you?"

I grin and wink. "New Orleans is a fun place for a young adult."

She squeaks and lightly punches my arm. "Red Light District is so different from red room."

"I don't know about that," I tease.

"I don't want to think about other girls you've fucked. Have you been tested?" she asks with even wider eyes. I can see the mischievous sparkle behind them, though.

I raise an eyebrow and smirk. "Many times."

She throws her head back and laughs. "You're such a dick. Why did I marry you?"

"Convenience. And because of my fingers." I hold up my middle and ring fingers and lick them.

She giggles and blushes a gorgeous shade of red as we finish putting things in the dishwasher. Every time she bends over, I lick my lips. Her ass is perfect. There's just enough to grab onto as I'm driving my cock into her.

I definitely notice she's checking me out just as much. As soon as we got to our hotel while in Switzerland, Skyla was all over me. I understood fully that she needed to feel me. All of me. She had to convince herself she was really safe. Since that day, she's woken up several times in the middle of the night needing to be held and feel all of me. I'm not a psychologist, but I know enough to know it's her way of convincing herself that everything is okay.

And then there are times like this when it's not out of a need. It's fully lust and desire for one another. A primal need deep within us both. Maybe it's to show love. Maybe it's nothing more than needing to fuck and be fucked.

As soon as I close the dishwasher door and hit the start button, my arms find her. I grip her ass and lift her as I plunge my tongue into her ready mouth. She wraps her legs around my waist and arms around my shoulders as she grinds herself into me.

That's all it takes.

All I need.

I sit her on the counter and tug her pajama bottoms off. I ferally tear her shirt clean off her as I'm pushing down my sweats. I've never been so happy that neither of us decided to get dressed in anything other than our pajamas. Not that we ever wear them in bed, but they get their use on lazy days like this.

Skyla groans when her shirt is torn from her body and sucks lightly on my tongue as she grips my dick. She gives it a couple of tugs and has me about ready to explode.

I pull her back into me. I'd intended to get my fill of her, but I'm not lasting long. I'll have to make it up to her. She wraps back around me as I pull her off the counter. Our tongues fight for a dominance she knows is all mine as I drop her on my waiting length.

"Oh! Dane!" Her nails dig into my shoulders as her head falls back. Her pussy grips my dick like a vice.

I grip her ass tighter and pull her into my hard and punishing thrusts. "Fuck, yes." My lips meet the sensitive flesh of her throat. I suck lightly, a contrast to the pace I'm pounding her.

She's so wet. Tight. Her pussy pulses and clenches for me. She moans and mumbles incoherently. I wasn't wearing a shirt to begin with, but as her nails scratch across my back, I'm even more happy that I'm not. I love feeling her against my skin in any way I can get her.

Skyla uses her legs to slam herself harder onto me. I thrust into her like a starving man. I am. I'm starving for her. I can't get enough of her. Her touch. Taste. The way she feels when her pussy grips my dick. When her sweet essence drips down my balls.

"Ah! Dane!" Her thighs start to tremble, and I can't stop the possessive, caveman-like grunt that passes from my lips.

My dick thickens. Our lips meet in a kiss capable of burning the world to the ground. "Come," I command against her lips. I nip her lower lip before plunging my tongue into her mouth.

I swallow her scream as her entire body convulses. Her pussy spasms with her release. I thrust deep and hard into her as she comes. Once I feel her trembling slow, I ram my cock into her one last time and bury myself deep. I throw my head back and groan as I fill her pussy with all of me.

Our hips jerk against each other's as we pant gripping each other with all the strength we have. She buries her head in my neck, and I carry her back to our private little sanctuary.

For the rest of the night, I make the sweetest love to my wife. Once we're too exhausted to move, I pull the blanket over us. I wrap her in my arms and fall into a peaceful sleep.

Chapter Twenty Two

❧ Skyla ❧

(Three Months Later)

I spin around slowly in our bedroom in front of the floor length mirror. I blink rapidly and fan my eyes so I don't cry at the way I look in the silver, floor-length Christian Dior dress I'm wearing. It's a thin, satiny material that's light and moves with me. It gives me the perfect amount of cleavage while not being too revealing and making me uncomfortable.

One of the things I love so much about Dane is how dominant he is while not being a controlling asshole. We've fallen into this comfortable routine over the years where he makes sure I'm on track and don't have to make decisions I don't need to. He says it's to free up my brain for making company decisions and worry about things that are important. I've gotten so used to all he does for me that I'm not sure I could function on a day to day basis without him.

Not that I love him only for all of that. I love him for all he is with my entire being. I need him. But I can't deny how much I love that he picks out my outfits without a second thought. He bought this dress for me without me even knowing. It appeared on the bed while I was getting ready for our evening. He even purchased a pair of silver, leather, kitten-heel sandals by Prada to go with the incredible dress.

I've been looking forward to this day all year. It's close to Christmas, and Lance's gala is happening tonight. He called it the Interlaced with Hope & Scars Gala. The tickets this year were sold out. He put on a raffle at the Children's Hospital and drew names of five families who get to come as the Lucinio and Crane Family's personal guests. I'm bouncing with excitement at getting to meet them.

After touching up my sparkly diamond hair clip and perfecting my updo, I grab my small, black clutch and hurry to the stairs. Dane is waiting for me at the bottom, and I suddenly feel like a Disney princess.

"Well, don't you look like a vision?" Dane drawls. His eyes wander up and down my body.

I blush furiously and put my hand on the railing. I slowly make my way down the stairs giving him the same eye fucking he's giving me. "You don't look so bad yourself, Lieutenant."

He rumbles appreciatively. He's wearing a tux that's tailored to fit every muscle of his body. It's black with a black shirt, but he's wearing a silver tie to match my dress. I melt at the sight, which makes his sexy grin even wider.

Once I reach the bottom of the stairs, he holds out his hand and guides me the rest of the way. "I knew that dress would look incredible on you." He leans down and brushes his lips across mine ever so careful not to ruin my makeup.

"Thank you," I whisper shyly.

Dane glances at his watch. "I can't wait to rip it off you later, but right now, we have a gala to get to."

I giggle. "Promises, promises," I roll my eyes playfully knowing exactly what it will get me.

Just as I wanted him to, he tugs me into him. I hit his chest with mine hard and giggle again then moan when he slaps my ass. "Such a bad girl," he rumbles with a cocky grin.

"Hmm… guess you'll have to punish me." I reach down and rub his perfect length before cupping it in my hand and squeezing lightly.

He jerks into my hand and moans. "Fuck, my girl. What are you trying to do? Make it so we don't make it to the gala?" He squeezes my butt, earning himself a soft mewl.

"No, sir. I want to go to the gala. I just want you primed when we get home." I give his dick another squeeze with a giggle.

He swats my butt once more before he kisses me lightly and lets me go. "You're in for one fuck of a night. Prepare not to sleep." He takes my hand and leads me to the door.

"You mean I get to sleep in tomorrow and have a lazy movie weekend? Yummy. Yes, please."

Dane laughs heartily as he helps me into my coat. It's a cold night. There's not a lot of snow on the ground yet, but there's plenty of chill and ice. I'm a little afraid to walk out of the house wearing the shoes I am. I don't want to slip.

Dane, reading me as well as he always does, squeezes my hand after he slips his black tux jacket on and buttons it. "I got you, baby. Don't worry. I won't let you fall."

"Maybe I should put boots on and change when we get there."

Dane kisses the tip of my nose. "Trust me."

I smile up at him and nod. He gives me the sexy smile only I get to see as he turns to the door. He leads me out and carefully helps me with the difficult task of walking. He was out earlier salting the sidewalks, so I'm sure I won't slip, but I'd really rather not risk it.

"God, there's a lot of limos," I say with wide eyes as I cling to Dane.

He smiles and kisses my head as he stops next to ours. "We wanted to make sure we arrive in style. People expect this. And since there will be media there, Josh wanted to be absolutely certain we all look our best for Lance."

I smile as I slide in. Cole is already seated with his date. I've never met her, but she looks nice. Small with blonde hair like me. Austin is settled with Racheal, who has earned the trust of the Lucinio Family. I couldn't be happier because I really like her. She was informed that Dane and I started out in a fake marriage that was never really fake. She laughed hysterically about it and said she never once would have deemed what we have fake. She's very much right.

"Josh has each family being picked up in a limo. Look at this." Cole shows us his phone. Sure enough, each family is dressed in their best evening wear, provided by Josh and Ryan, I'm sure, and are happily posing outside their respective limos.

"Oh my God, that's adorable!" Racheal says with a huge smile.

I laugh. "Look at that one! They are all wearing pink!"

"That's Anneke. She just beat breast cancer. Her kids are actually really healthy, but Josh heard her story and wanted to extend an invite. She's a popular author. I guess Dallas reads all of her books, follows her on social media, and was telling Josh about her," Dane says. "I remember he was talking about helping her with her passport. I guess she was in another country. Her husband was here working. She fought it alone for the most part. He was able to be there for the surgery but had to go back before she finished her treatment. She had her kids and some friends and family there, but she had to feel pretty alone without the love of her life there. She was a fucking trooper, though. "

"Awe, that's both sad and amazing. Hopefully, it has a happy ending, and she gets to be with her husband for good," I say. "I'm really excited to meet everyone."

The driver starts driving as Cole puts his phone away. I settle next to Dane and smile as everyone talks about the gala and how excited they are. I can't wait to see all the decorations. I know that Raleigh, Lance, and Rosie were working hard at making everything perfect.

As soon as we arrive, I see all of the media. For a brief moment, I start looking around for Thurston or any of his assholes watching for me. I tense just enough for Dane to feel. He squeezes my shoulder soothingly and leans in. He kisses my cheek, and it's then I remember everything is over. The tension fully releases.

"The plan is to get the family inside before the other families arrive. We want them to have a red carpet moment and be greeted by us when they enter," Dane says as the driver opens the door for us. He scoots out and holds his hand out for me. I take it, and he kisses it as I get out. I blush when the media cheers and snaps pictures. "A moment fit for a queen," he whispers in my ear.

I smile brightly as he leads me into the venue. We're followed closely by Austin and Racheal, then Cole and his date. I still haven't gotten her name, but I'm not sure I want it anymore. She didn't seem too excited to see the families that Cole showed us. I'm pretty sure I saw her roll her eyes.

"Oh my God, Dane," I say when we get inside. Ryan is already here with most of his family. So is Josh and most of the Lucinio family.

But it's the room that has me spinning in a slow circle with my mouth agape and wide eyes. The table cloths are silver. There are dark purple vases with light purple lilies in them. There are candles floating in water-filled, purple, glass bowls. It takes me a minute to see the candles aren't real, but they certainly look it.

Above us are purple and white fairy lights and silver chandeliers that sparkle with the light. The ambiance of the room is so calming and elegant that it takes my breath away. They've even got purple accent walls.

When my eyes land on one table near the stage, though, my emotions nearly spill over. I know instantly who it's for. It's got a silver table cloth, just like the rest of the room, but the vase is pink. The flowers are pink. The candles and the glass bowl are pink. I know it must be for our breast cancer survivor.

"Everything looks incredible," Dane says as he wraps his arms around me.

Several minutes later, after we greet all of our personal guests and talk to them a little bit, other guests start to arrive. I notice several of Chicago's elite and can't help but feel honored that they've shown up for such an amazing cause, even if they probably will use their donation as a tax write-off.

I stand next to Raleigh as Dane grabs us both something to drink. She's wearing a gorgeous purple dress. I notice that all of us women in the Crane and Lucinio families are wearing either silver or purple. I have a feeling it was intentional and a detail Dane knew and didn't worry about telling me because he was picking my outfit. Honestly, though, I love that he didn't tell me because it's a detail that seeing in front of me is a sweet surprise.

"Welcome to the Interlaced with Hope and Scars Gala!" Lance booms from the stage. His smile is so pure and genuine. Anyone can tell he's proud of the turnout. "If you all will start taking your seats, we'll get started. Each seat will have a name placard on it." Everyone begins moving. Dane appears and takes my hand. He leads both me and Raleigh to a table with Alex, Josh, and some other girl I've never seen before in my life.

"While you all are getting settled, let me take a second to introduce the two of us," Damon says. He stands next to his beaming husband. "I'm

Damon. This is my husband, Lance, the mastermind behind this entire thing."

Lance smiles. "I had a lot of help."

Damon winks at him. "We have a few guests of honor here." Damon begins introducing each family.

I spot Josh glaring toward another table. I furrow my brows and glance at Dane. He's got the same confused expression on his face and follows Josh's furious gaze. I look where he is and raise an eyebrow. Dallas is sitting at a table with Rosie and two guys probably about their age. I nibble my lip and look back at Dane in confusion. He shrugs just as bewildered as me.

Alex leans over and whispers something to Josh as Dane drops his hand to my thigh and gently squeezes. Josh's expression doesn't soften, but he does look away from Dallas. I glance back over at Dallas. She looks down the second she sees me, but her expression looks pained.

"Okay, what's happening?" I whisper to Dane.

"Your guess is as good as mine, baby," he whispers back.

My mind starts thinking of all of the possibilities of whatever is happening. I'm quiet all through dinner as I think. Even while the silent auction and dance is happening, I'm completely lost in thought. But even after everything, I can't think of anything that's remotely a possibility for those looks between them except for one thing.

And that one thing is heartbreaking.

"Let's dance," Dane says, squeezing my hand and immediately erasing all of my thoughts.

I shake my head and stare at him in shock. "You didn't just say that. You hate dancing."

"True. I do. But ever since our first dance at our reception a couple months ago, I can't stop thinking about how good you feel in my arms while we're swaying back and forth to a slow song." There's a dangerous and very sexy twinkle that looks to set his beautiful jade eyes on fire. It's not something I have the power to resist. I don't want to anyway.

I follow him to the dance floor, my hand in his. His thumb slides back and forth over the back of my hand. The simple touch sends goosebumps up my arm and heat to my core. When we reach the edge of the floor, he pulls me into him. His arms lock tight around me, and he starts swaying to the music. I don't even know the song that's playing; if it's fast or slow because all I can think about is the way his body feels against mine.

A few kisses later, Dane spins me out from his body and back in. My back hits his chest. I gasp at the feel of his hardness against my lower back. His lips meet my neck. He leaves soft kisses across the side of it as his arms keep me tight against him. There's no mistaking how hard he is.

When it's impossible for me to take anymore, I take his hand. I quickly walk towards the area where we checked our coats. I remember there being a closet that I have every intention of making really good use of.

Dane follows me, amused, and I suddenly feel like a teenager sneaking out of my house to do something naughty. I can't help but giggle as I lead him down the empty hallway just past the coat check. I tug him into the closet with me and turn on the light as I close the door.

"What are you doing, pretty girl?" Dane asks with a cocky grin.

"No way you don't know what I'm doing." I look around for something I can put on the ground so I don't wreck my pretty dress. I see a folded blanket and drop it on the ground. The staff will just have to wash it. I hike my dress up as I drop to my knees.

Dane reaches over and locks the door. The cocky grin drops from his face the second I reach for his belt. "Baby, you're gonna get us caught."

"Danger." I giggle and look up at him as I unzip his fly. "Makes it so much more sexy."

"Fuck, Sky." He moans when I pull his dick out of his boxer briefs. His hand circles the back of my neck, and he pushes me closer to him.

I kitten lick his dick before taking it into my mouth. He's too big for me to get all eight or nine inches in my mouth, but the second he touches the back of my throat, I swallow. Bobbing my head back and forth, I pump his cock with my hand as I suck and lick him. I rotate my wrist at the same frantic pace I'm moving my head.

"Mmm…," I moan quietly, but enough to send vibrations through him.

"Fuck," he whispers as his dick jerks.

I reach up with my other hand and start playing with his balls. I've learned very well that the second I do it, his dick almost always gets thick.

This time is no different, and I smile. I roll his balls in my hand as they harden and draw up. His dick thickens. He groans.

"Mmm…," I moan softly once more.

"Fuck, I'm gonna come," he rumbles.

I keep my eyes on his as I suck. I flick my tongue rapidly over his thick length and suck harder. Each time he hits the back of my throat, I swallow around him. I keep stroking his cock and rolling his balls in my palm.

His hand shakes just as little before he starts coming down my throat. He watches me as I swallow. I can't stop my eyes from rolling back and closing as I thirstily drink all he has to give me.

When he finishes, I lick him clean. He gives me a low, appreciative groan as he helps me to my feet. Before he even tucks himself away, he adjusts my dress and makes sure I look perfect.

"We should probably get back out there," I say with a soft blush.

Dane leans down and kisses me until he has to pull back for the sake of breathing. He licks his lip. "The night's almost over. When we get home…" He trails off. The promise in his eyes as he tucks himself away makes me shiver.

I look down at the blanket and pick it up. "I feel bad I selfishly used this so I didn't get dirty."

He takes it and opens the door. He takes my hand and leads me out. He sees someone at the coat check in. The young kid, a male just grins as he takes the blanket and winks.

"I'll take care of it, sir. Enjoy the rest of the gala."

"Thanks, man," Dane says. I say nothing, too shocked for words.

The only explanation for that is bro code. That's what that was. I can't help but giggle as I follow Dane back to the gala.

The rest of the night goes quickly. When we're finished and everyone is leaving, I catch Josh using sign language to speak to a kid. He's kneeling down so he's eye level with the kid. Both have huge smiles on their faces as they sign excitedly. I don't know what they're saying, but it's completely adorable. The kid's parents look like they might actually cry.

I catch Dallas on the other side of the room looking at Josh with a mixture of so much love and pain that I can feel it deep in my soul. Whatever is going on is quickly forgotten when Dane kisses me and helps me put my coat on. He leads me to our limo with a promise of an unforgettable night.

Sex aside, I'd follow this man to the ends of the Earth if he led me there.

Chapter Twenty Three

☙ Dane ❧

(One Month Later)

I grip Skyla's hips and watch her sweet pussy take my entire length. I don't know what's gotten into either of us today, but this isn't the first time we've found ourselves like this. This morning I had her on the kitchen counter. Not an hour later, she had me on the floor of the living room. I just had her bent over the couch, creamed her, then pulled her on top of me to give her the ride of her life.

"Christ, you look so good dripping down my dick." I tug her hair and pull her to my lips before she has a chance to say anything.

She moans and moves her hands to my shoulders from the back of the couch. She grips them tight as she bounces up and down. I love the way her tits move with her. So much so that when I break the kiss, I take one of her nipples in my mouth and suck. Hard.

"Ah! Dane!" Her pussy pulses and clenches over and over again with each thrust I give her. I slam her down on top of me so I sink deeper and deeper.

Of all the positions I've had her in, Cowgirl is my favorite. Nothing on her body is hidden. I get to enjoy all of her. The way she takes my dick. The way she loses control and her hands run through her hair. The way her thighs tremble for me when she's getting close. The way her eyes darken just before she comes.

There's nothing like the feeling of knowing that I'm giving my girl everything she needs. That every movement is showing her how I feel. Feeling the way she responds to me when I do. When I feel her start to spasm uncontrollably around my dick, I adjust my grip on her thighs and spread them wider, allowing me to sink impossibly deeper.

My eyes roll back at the feel of her pussy gripping me so exquisitely. "One more, sexy girl. Give me one more," I rumble against her neck as I roll my hips. "Come for me, baby. Soak me. Show me who this pussy belongs to." I thrust deep one last time as I continue rolling my hips, knowing my tip rubs against her spot over and over again.

Words fail her. All that comes out of her mouth is moans, screams, and maybe my name. I hold her still while her whole body jerks and trembles as she releases. Her nails scratch my shoulders, marking her territory, and sending shivers of desire and possessiveness through me. They find their way back into her hair as she slowly starts coming down.

Then, and only then, do I come hard and deep inside her. I pull her down so I can kiss her as, once again, our hips jerk against each other's. Our tongue's slide over one another's as her pussy greedily drinks me. She clenches tight around me. I've learned it's her way of keeping me and my come inside her as long as possible.

"Fuck...," I rumble into her hair as our chests heave against each other's. I keep my fingers tangled in her golden locks.

She nuzzles into my neck murmuring something incoherently. I smile and hold her close with my lips pressed against her neck.

"I'm so in love with you," she whispers.

"I'm so in love with you, too," I rumble low as I kiss her neck.

"Come on, Dane!" someone shouts in a growly, but high-pitched voice.

Skyla jumps. Her eyes dart to the open door of the den. I raise an eyebrow and hug her closer. I know it's one of my asshole brothers. Just need to figure out which one is getting his ass kicked.

"What the fuck do you want? I'm busy," I growl.

Cole laughs and appears in the doorway of the den with his back turned. "We got an urgent mission, Lieutenant. So, get your pinkie out of her hooha, and move your ass!"

I roll my eyes. "Do you not believe in phone calls? Or, I don't know. Knocking on the fucking door?"

"I tried the phone thing. You didn't answer. As for knocking, I would've done that. Except I knew if you didn't answer your phone, you probably had Skyla bent over something."

"Cole!" Skyla shrieks. I grab our fleece from the back of the couch and wrap it around her as I guide her off me. We both groan at the loss.

"Go outside," I tell him. "Or somewhere not in my line of sight if you don't want to see my ass naked."

Cole huffs like the dick he is. I know it's teasing, but I bite down the laugh. "I waited patiently for you to finish... twice. We gotta go!" Cole walks away. The pillow I throw at him barely misses his back as he laughs.

"He better not have seen me naked."

I stand but lean down and kiss my flushed wife. "He would've stopped in his tracks when he heard us. I promise."

She narrows her eyes. "When I get my hands on him, he's a dead man."

I laugh as I jog out of the den. I wouldn't put it past her to try. I take the stairs two at a time and run directly to the bathroom in our bedroom. I clean up quickly before getting dressed. After I get my usual jeans and black, long-sleeve shirt on, I grab my bulletproof vest. I strap it on and quickly grab both of my guns. I strap one to my leg. The other goes in the holster at my hip.

Once I finish, I jog downstairs and grab the rest of my gear after putting on my black SWAT boots. It's a chilly January night, so I grab a coat. I'll see what the mission is before I go any further with dressing the part.

I jump in Cole's truck and throw my gear in the back next to his. "What's up?"

"Gavin texted a little while ago. Said to grab you and the team. Meet him by the docks. No more details." Cole takes off. "I almost interrupted you, but he gave me a time to be there."

I take that as my cue to call Damon. If Gavin is in position somewhere, I don't want to disturb that. We have protocols we follow. If we don't, just like on my job, people could get hurt or killed. I put the phone on speaker so Cole can hear.

"North side. All the way to the end," Damon commands the second he answers. "I need law enforcement to cover our ass on this one."

"What's going on? What do you need from us?"

"I need you and your team to meet up with Gavin. I'm with Lance in the building across from where you'll be. You'll see one light in the building you're hitting. That room has a kid. Young. Maybe three or five. I don't know. Three guards inside the room. One outside the room. Lance has heat signatures in several parts of the building. Gavin knows where. I need you to go directly for the kid. He's in the middle of the top floor. Six floors."

"Got it," I say. "Who does he belong to?"

"Don't know. I got a text from a number I don't recognize. All it said was the kid is in the warehouse. Gave me an address. Then said they don't know who else to contact. They said they'd meet me here. I'm waiting before we make any moves." He pauses, and I hear shuffling before some murmured voices. A few moments later, he comes back on the line. "Contact doesn't know who the kid is, but he's been held captive on a ship for years. I can tell you the kid looks malnourished and dirty. He's not being taken care of."

I narrow my eyes. "On a ship? Like a cargo ship?"

"Yes. And don't talk to me about the Coast Guard. I'll take care of them."

I shake my head. "It's not that, man. He's on land. Jurisdiction is mine, but this investigation will probably end up getting handed to Feds if that ship is from somewhere else in the US. If it's international, we're fucked. The Feds will take it if it's in a country they're allowed to be in, but this is likely going to Interpol."

"Josh is already on the Feds. He pulled Luke to get him in with the ATF. They're talking to them right now, but we need to do this quick. Something about this doesn't feel right to any of us. The second I told Josh, he instantly thought human trafficking."

I rub my head. "Keep the Feds off me on this one. The second this case gets to them, contacts ain't gonna matter. We have some pretty good information that human trafficking goes far up the line with them. I've been working on it when I have time, and I've found a lot of shit."

"I got your back. I'll take care of it. I'll text Josh right now."

"If you want to pull Feds, the ATF is a safe bet. Keep the FBI, Homeland, and the CIA off this."

"Understood."

I hang up and text my team with the position I need them. "This is going to be a mess."

"First thing is getting that kid. Text our lab contact. He can be waiting for us when we show up. We can draw some blood and hopefully get a match to a relative or something."

"Good idea." I quickly send the text as Cole pulls up near the warehouses. We stay far away from the one we need to be at. No way we want anyone aware we're coming.

We both get out and open his back doors. We quickly grab the gear we need, including a black ski mask and AR-15 with silencers for our weapons. We put them on and swiftly make our way to our meeting place. As soon as we get there, Gavin is sending in teams. I'm pleased to see my team is already here. I nod a thank you to Cole for getting them going.

Gavin looks at me. "I need you and your team with me. We're going for the kid," he says quietly. "We need to be in and out in less than three minutes. Any longer, we risk the Coast Guard being called in. Not that we can't deal with them, but it means wasted and lost time. I want to avoid it at all costs."

"Where's the people in the building?" Cole asks before I can.

"Everywhere, man." He turns a tablet towards us. "We have 4 teams. One will be taking the stairs in the middle. One will take the side. We'll be taking the Northernmost side. Team four stays out here surrounding the building. They watch out for us. In the unlikely event someone gets out, they take them down. We call out numbers. If we take out ten, we say ten. Lance and Damon are keeping track and watching for any surprise heat signatures we don't see. No shots fired. Josh wants everyone."

I nod. "Got it. Let's go." I take my position behind Gavin as he turns and signals for everyone to move.

In a near silent and dark mass of bodies, everyone moves. We quickly take up our positions and wait for Gavin to give us the signal as he hands me and Cole our earpieces. We both put them on and ready ourselves. Cole uses his AR-15. I choose my Glock.

"Enter," Gavin growls.

We've chosen not to bust down doors. Our entrance is as quiet as it can be. As soon as we enter, there's a staircase to our left. According to what Gavin showed us, there's a target near our entrance. We all keep our guard up. I see him first. He's leaning against the wall looking at his phone. I put him in a sleeper hold. Seconds later, he's down, cuffed, and gagged with his legs bound to his arms so he can't go anywhere.

We climb the stairs and quickly do the same to each guard we come across calling out how many we take each time. By the time we get to the top, everyone on the bottom floors has been subdued.

"Coming up on two minutes," Damon says. "No call for Coast Guard, but hurry the fuck up. I see a guard doing his rounds. Coming right for you."

"Fuck," I grumble.

"Two," Cole calls over the radio, telling them the two guards we just took down.

"No one near you," Lance says. "Team two and three have everyone else subdued. Only people left are those in the room."

Gavin positions himself on one side of the door. Aiden takes the other. He's always been our best lead entrance team member. He also loves it, and I'd hate to deny him his fun.

"Team two in position," someone says over the earpieces.

"Team three in position," another person says. Gavin mumbles an acknowledgement.

"All accounted for," Lance says. "Everyone you took out is still down. No movement."

"Copy," Gavin growls. "Three… two… one…" Gavin and Aiden kick the door in, causing immediate screaming from the child and adults.

Me, Gavin, Cole, Aiden, and Lucas all rush the guards as Aimee moves directly for the child to comfort him.

There's no heat in the building, and he's wearing the thinnest, most tattered clothing I've ever seen. They are way too small. His toes are coming out of his shoes. I can see my breath in the air. I'm not cold because of the adrenaline, and movement, but this poor kid has to be nearing hypothermia. The guards are all wearing very warm clothing, and it pisses me right off.

Aimee immediately removes her lightweight jacket. It might not be the thickest and warmest, but it's better than nothing. I'm glad she thought to wear it. Her body heat will keep him a little warmer.

"I have the little one," she says softly into the earpiece. She lifts him as she hugs him. "Shh, sweet one. You're safe now… It's okay… Shh…" She nuzzles him.

"Get out, guys. Guard is close."

"Team four has him, but if he doesn't check in, we'll have cops and guards all over. Let's move," someone from team four says.

Aimee miraculously gets the little boy to calm down, but I know she's not going to be able to carry him the whole way. She's a small girl. Tough as nails, but I can already see she's struggling a little bit holding him. He's malnourished for sure, but he's still not that light.

"Here. Let me take him," I say quietly. I rub the kid's back hoping to help stop the shivering. "That okay with you, little man? Let's get you warm, dressed, and fed. How's that sound?"

The boy looks at me. He studies me for several moments while Gavin commands the other teams to start moving our prisoners out. He decides that I'm trustworthy and holds out his arms.

"How about a piggyback ride?" Aimee asks with a smile. The boy tilts his head, and we both realize that he has no idea what that is. I turn my back to him with a smile. "See, you wrap your arms around the nice policeman's shoulders. And then you wrap your legs around his waist." She helps put her jacket on him instead of just having him wrapped in it, then adjusts him so he can do as she says. He eagerly does it like he's excited to learn something new.

Once we have him settled, we all leave the room and exit the building quickly. With little to no words, we hurry back to our vehicles and get the fuck out of dodge. I don't need the paperwork that would come with dock guards and the Coast Guard showing up.

"Yeah, baby, it won't be long. I'm just waiting on a call from the lab. Cole said he was just about finished up." I lean back in my desk chair and hold my phone between my shoulder and my ear.

"What about the little one?" Skyla asks me with a yawn.

"We'll probably keep him for a few days. I'm hoping to find a relative we can contact tonight, though."

"Don't you guys just get criminals with the DNA stuff when you check? I would hate for him to be saved only to be put back into the hands of someone he shouldn't be."

"Valid concern. But we have access to DNA from a long list of sources. Not just the criminals."

She's quiet for a few moments before I hear her yawn again. "Did you get him to talk at all yet?"

"I get nods out of him. Or head shakes. No words. Whenever I ask his name or what people call him, he shrugs or just looks down at the ground." I look at my watch when I see our lab expert, Pete, appear at my door. I put my finger to my lips when he walks in and point to the boy who is lying on my couch. "It's three in the morning, baby. Go to sleep. I'll be home soon."

"I can stay up," she murmurs.

I chuckle. "Sleep, sweet girl. I love you."

"Love you…," she whispers.

I smile as I hang up. "What do you got?" I ask, my voice just as low as it was when I was talking to Skyla.

Pete hands me the paperwork as he sits down. He glances over his shoulder. "He definitely looks a lot warmer and content with new clothes that actually fit him. Looks pretty good, cleaned up."

"Familiar. He looks familiar." I glance up and narrow my eyes when Pete stays silent. "What?"

Pete clears his throat. "I ran him through everything I could think of. Nothing came back with anything conclusive. So, I ran him through adoption agencies. Hospitals. Literally anything I could think of." He pauses and nods to the papers. "I finally got a hit."

I flip to the last page, eager to see what he found, but what I see isn't at all what I was expecting. I shake my head and thrust the papers at him. "That's not possible. Run it again."

"I did, Lieutenant. Five times." His eyes lock on mine. "We also found him in Missing Persons. It was a report filed six years ago." He rifles through the papers in front of me and shows me the report.

My mind races with every single possibility I can think of as I scan it. None of them make any more sense than the one that I previously came up with. It all has my eyes flicking between the boy and the papers. I shake my head several more times before the full reality of this situation hits me like a fucking truck.

But my mind still refuses to fully believe it.

It's not fucking possible. It just isn't.

"Police. Run his DNA against any police officer who has ever given a sample at any time."

"Lieutenant, I did. I ran his DNA through everything. CODIS. Everything, sir. I might not be able to go as far as Lucinio Mafia or something, but I don't think there are more DNA databases in the world than what I've run it through. Unless there's secret government shit."

"I wouldn't put it past them," I growl low with a sigh. I tap my finger against the papers. "Conclusive?"

"Ninety-nine-point-nine percent."

We both look over at the sleeping boy. I knew there was something way too familiar about him. His eyes are a piercing blue. Fucking dangerous. His facial features are both sharp and soft. Despite the shit he's obviously been through, there's a bravery inside him that forces him to stand tall. He has a button nose, long lashes, and a smile that's very familiar, but a smirk that's even more well-known to me.

While part of me is glad that this kid is safe, another part of me is fearful of what him being found will mean. It's not something I want to bring Josh. I know I need to, but I don't know what this will do to him.

It's something that will either strengthen him and make him whole...

...or destroy us all irrevocably.

The End

Next In The Lucinio Family Series

The devilishly dark and alluring Lucinio Family Series continues with *Phoenix Rising*.

Dangerous. Vindictive. Ruthless. Fearless. Demonic. Satanic. Satan himself. Mafia King.

All words that describe me, Lucinio Mafia's leader. The boss. I've taken my family name to heights not even I dared to dream of.

Very few know the price I've paid to get here. They don't know the darkness I crawl out of every single day for the sake of my family; my name. It's that darkness, the evil inside, that keeps me as guarded as I am.

Especially against her.

Dallas Cassidy is barely more than a girl. She's the princess of Viper's Venom, a motorcycle club with a reputation just as vicious as mine. The little sister of the leader of VV, who just happens to be my best friend.

No one has been able to bust down my walls the way she has, but she's way too good for a man like me. I'll ruin her.

One sentence that rocks me and my entire family to our core has the blackness in my soul taking complete control. I want nothing more than to destroy the entire world with my wrath alone.

To protect the woman who owns me from being incinerated by the flames chasing me down, I put more and more distance between her and the demons that live inside me. Only, I know I need her love. I won't survive without it.

~ Phoenix Rising is a dark, mafia, age gap, brother's best friend, best friend's little sister romance with violent themes and adult content that may not be suitable for all readers. ~

Order your copy of *Phoenix Rising* today!

The Lucinio Family Series

Available Now

Other Books By Melony Ann
The Beautiful Dream Series

Available Now

Loving You
My Love, My Heart
Softening Lyric
Undercover Temptations
Captain Charming
Breaking Boundaries
Crashing Into You
Tactical Inferno
Ravishing Our Queen
Cherished By The Texan
Unveiling Our Passions

Box Sets Available

The Beautiful Dream Series: Box Set: Part 1
The Beautiful Dream Series: Box Set: Part 2

The Crane Family Series

Available Now

Box Sets Available

The Deimos Trilogy

Available Now

Box Sets Available

The Forbidden Temptation Series

Available Now

Multi Author Series
Piper Falls: Firehouse 49

Available Now

Ignite My Fire by Melony Ann
Regain My Fire by Kindra White
Playing With My Fire by D.L. Howe
Fight My Fire by Darley Collins
Against My Fire by Anneke Boshoff
Relight My Fire by Louise Murchie
Harness My Fire by Ayana Lisbet
Quench My Fire by Havana Wilder

Let's Be Friends

Follow me on

Bookbub

Facebook

Goodreads

Instagram

Tik Tok

Visit my website
www.melonyannauthor.com

Subscribe to my newsletter and get a FREE never-seen-before NOVELLA just for subscribers!
https://www.melonyannauthor.com/exclusive-content

Join my Facebook Reader Group!
Jason's and Melony's Sizzling Book Nook

The official Lucinio Family Series Playlist on YouTube
https://youtube.com/playlist?list=PLGEiD5wbQmDdjFYhMKrFsomQOTrRK7x9Y

Dedication

Your soul is in the wind, the rain, and the air we breathe. Whenever we feel alone, you're there.

Acknowledgements

Brad - You stopped my heart from shattering and are still by my side. I don't know what possessed you to take me on, but it will be something I'll forever be in your debt for. I love you.

Laura - Knowing all I know about you now, I can't believe you were brave enough to pop into my DMs just to tell me you loved my books. All of these years later, we've become a power couple. I love you.

Jay - I still can't believe we started on a Delta flight in Duluth when I honestly believed I was going to die. All these years later, you're still here making sure I don't die. I love you.

Ayana - Thank you for being the sweet soul that you are.

Anneke - You're the true, real life Superwoman. I'm honored to call you my friend, and even more honored to call you my chosen family. I love you.

Jason - To think a year ago I didn't know who you were. Now, I can't imagine my life without you in it. I love you.

To the Bookstagram Community.

To my family.

To all of those who believe in me and support me.

To all of those who don't.

Cover by: Carter Cover Designs

Edited by: Alyssa Skaggs

About Melony Ann

Melony Ann began writing short stories and poetry as a child. She continued honing her craft over the years until she took the plunge and began publishing her work, despite having severe anxiety.

Melony writes contemporary romance stories that are full of suspense and a lot of steam.

When she isn't writing, she is loving her family and working to make her life something she deserves.

Melony believes that if her writing can inspire just one person, then all of her hard work is worth it.

Her hope is that her writing allows each and every one of her readers to escape for a little while. To dive into a different world one book at a time.